Wesker took a single step toward the slaughter in front of them—

—when all around, deep, echoing howls filled the warm night air, shrill voices of predatorial fury coming at the S.T.A.R.S. from all directions.

"Back to the 'copter, *now!*" Wesker shouted.

Chris ran, Barry and Jill in front of him and Wesker bringing up the rear. The four of them sprinted through dark trees, unseen branches slapping at them as the howls grew louder, more insistent.

Wesker turned and fired blindly into the woods as they stumbled toward the waiting helicopter, its blades already spinning. Chris felt relief sweep through him; Brad must have heard the shots. They still had a chance. . . .

Chris could hear the creatures behind them now, the sharp rustling of lean, muscular bodies tearing through the trees. He could also see Brad's pale, wide-eyed face through the glass front of the 'copter, the reflected lights of the control panel casting a greenish glow across his panicked features. He was shouting something, but the roar of the engine drowned out everything now, the blast of wind churning the field into a rippling sea.

Another fifty feet, almost there—

Suddenly, the helicopter jerked into the air, accelerating wildly. Chris caught a final glimpse of Brad's face and could see the blind terror there, the unthinking panic that had gripped him as he clawed at the controls.

"*No! Don't go!*" Chris screamed, but the wobbling rails were already out as the 'copter pitching forward and away from darkness.

They were going to

D0920070

Also by S.D. Perry

RESIDENT EVIL: THE UMBRELLA CONSPIRACY
RESIDENT EVIL: CALIBAN COVE
RESIDENT EVIL: CITY OF THE DEAD
RESIDENT EVIL: UNDERWORLD
RESIDENT EVIL: NEMESIS
RESIDENT EVIL: CODE:VERONICA

Published by POCKET BOOKS

RESIDENT EVIL

THE UMBRELLA CONSPIRACY

S.D. PERRY

POCKET BOOKS
New York   London   Toronto   Sydney

For information regarding special discounts for bulk purchases, please contact Simon & Schuster Special Sales at 1-800-456-6798 or business@simonandschuster.com

This book is a work of fiction. Names, characters, places and incidents are products of the author's imagination or are used fictitiously. Any resemblance to actual events or locales or persons, living or dead, is entirely coincidental.

An *Original* Publication of POCKET BOOKS

POCKET BOOKS, a division of Simon & Schuster, Inc.
1230 Avenue of the Americas, New York, NY 10020

ISBN: 0-671-02439-6

First Pocket Books printing October 1998

20   19   18   17   16   15

POCKET and colophon are registered trademarks of Simon & Schuster, Inc.

Cover art by Gerber Studio

Printed in the U.S.A.

For Mÿk, so far.

Evil events from evil causes spring.

—Aristophanes

THE UMBRELLA
CONSPIRACY

PROLOGUE

Latham Weekly, June 2, 1998

BIZARRE MURDERS COMMITTED IN RACCOON CITY

RACCOON CITY—The mutilated body of forty-two-year-old Anna Mitaki was discovered late yesterday in an abandoned lot not far from her home in northwest Raccoon City, making her the fourth victim of the supposed "cannibal killers" to be found in or near the Victory Lake district in the last month. Consistent with the coroner reports of the other recent victims, Mitaki's corpse showed evidence of having been partially eaten, the bite patterns apparently formed by human jaws.

Shortly after the discovery of Miss Mitaki by two joggers at approximately nine o'clock last night, Chief Irons made a brief statement insisting that the RPD is "working diligently to apprehend the perpetrators of such heinous crimes" and that he is currently consulting with city officials about more drastic protection measures for Raccoon citizens.

In addition to the murderous spree of the cannibal killers, three others have died from probable animal attacks in Raccoon Forest in the past several weeks, bringing the toll of mysterious deaths up to seven. . . .

Raccoon Times, June 22, 1998

HORROR IN RACCOON!
MORE VICTIMS DEAD

RACCOON CITY—The bodies of a young couple were found early Sunday morning in Victory Park, making Deanne Rusch and Christopher Smith the eighth and ninth victims in the reign of violence that has terrorized the city since mid-May of this year.

Both victims, aged 19, were reported as missing by concerned parents late Saturday night and were discovered by police officers on the west bank of Victory Lake at approximately 2 A.M. Although no formal statement has been issued by the police department, witnesses to the discovery confirm that both youths suffered wounds similar to those found on prior victims. Whether or not the attackers were human or animal has yet to be announced.

According to friends of the young couple, the two had talked about tracking down the rumored "wild dogs" recently spotted in the heavily forested park and had planned to violate the city-wide curfew in order to see one of the alleged nocturnal creatures.

Mayor Harris has scheduled a press conference for this afternoon, and is expected to make an announcement regarding the current crisis, calling for a stricter enforcement of the curfew. . . .

Cityside, July 21, 1998

"S.T.A.R.S." SPECIAL TACTICS AND RESCUE
SQUAD SENT TO SAVE RACCOON CITY

RACCOON CITY—With the reported disappearance of three hikers in Raccoon Forest earlier this week, city officials have finally called for a roadblock on rural Route 6 at the foothills of the Arklay Mountains. Police Chief Brian Irons announced yesterday that the S.T.A.R.S. will participate full-time in the search for the hikers and will also be working closely with the RPD until there is an end to the rash of murders and disappearances that are destroying our community.

Chief Irons, a former S.T.A.R.S. member himself, said today (in an exclusive *Cityside* telephone interview) that it is "high time to employ the talents of these dedicated men and women toward the safety of this city. We've had nine brutal murders here in less than two months, and at least five disappearances now—and all of these events have taken place in a close proximity to Raccoon Forest. This leads us to believe that the perpetrators of these crimes may be hiding somewhere in the Victory Lake district, and the S.T.A.R.S. have just the kind of experience we need to find them."

When asked why the S.T.A.R.S. hadn't been assigned to these cases until now, Chief Irons would only say that the S.T.A.R.S. have been assisting the RPD since the beginning and that they would be a "welcome addition" to the task force currently working on the murders full-time.

Founded in New York in 1967, the privately funded S.T.A.R.S. organization was originally created as a measure against cult-affiliated terrorism by a group of retired military officials and ex-field operatives from both the CIA and FBI. Under the guidance of former NSDA (National Security and Defense Agency) director Marco Palmieri, the group quickly expanded its services to include everything from hostage negotiation to code breaking to riot control. Working with local police agencies, each branch office of the S.T.A.R.S. is designed to work as a complete unit in itself. The S.T.A.R.S. set up its Raccoon City branch through the fund-raising efforts of several local businesses in 1972 and is currently led by Captain Albert Wesker, promoted to the position less than six months ago. . . .

Oпе

JILL WAS ALREADY LATE FOR THE BRIEFING
when she somehow managed to drop her keys into her
cup of coffee on the way out the door. There was a
muted *ting* as they hit the bottom, and as she paused
in mid-stride, staring in disbelief at the steaming
ceramic mug, the thick stack of files she carried under
her other arm slid smoothly to the floor. Paper clips
and sticky notes scattered across the tan carpeting.

"Ah, *shit.*"

She checked her watch as she turned back toward
the kitchen, cup in hand. Wesker had called the
meeting for 1900 sharp, which meant she had about
nine minutes to make the ten-minute drive, find
parking and get her butt into a chair. The first full
disclosure meeting since the S.T.A.R.S. had gotten

the case—hell, the first real meeting since she'd made the Raccoon transfer—and she was going to be late.

Figures. Probably the first time in years I actually give a rat's ass about being on time and I fall apart at the door. . . .

Muttering darkly she hurried to the sink, feeling tense and angry with herself for not getting ready earlier. It was the case, the goddamn case. She'd picked up her copies of the ME files right after breakfast and spent all day digging through the reports, searching for something that the cops had somehow missed—and feeling more and more frustrated as the day slipped past and she'd failed to come up with anything new.

She dumped the mug and scooped up the warm, wet keys, wiping them against her jeans as she hurried back to the front door. She crouched down to gather the files—and stopped, staring down at the glossy color photo that had ended up on top.

Oh, girls. . . .

She picked it up slowly, knowing that she didn't have time and yet unable to look away from the tiny, blood-spattered faces. She felt the knots of tension that had been building all day intensify, and for a moment it was all she could do to breathe as she stared at the crime scene photo. Becky and Priscilla McGee, ages nine and seven. She'd flipped past it earlier, telling herself that there was nothing there she needed to see. . . .

. . . But it isn't true, is it? You can keep pretending, or you can admit it—everything's different now, it's been different since the day they died.

When she'd first moved to Raccoon, she'd been under a lot of stress, feeling uncertain about the transfer, not even sure if she wanted to stay with the S.T.A.R.S. She was good at the job, but had only taken it because of Dick; after the indictment, he'd started to pressure her to get into another line of work. It had taken awhile, but her father was persistent, telling her again and again that one Valentine in jail was one too many, even admitting that he was wrong to raise her the way he had. With her training and background, there weren't a whole lot of options—but the S.T.A.R.S., at least, appreciated her skills and didn't care how she came by them. The pay was decent, there was the element of risk she'd grown to enjoy. . . . In retrospect, the career change had been surprisingly easy; it made Dick happy, and gave her the opportunity to see how the other half lived.

Still, the move had been harder on her than she'd realized. For the first time since Dick had gone inside, she'd felt truly alone, and working for the law had started to seem like a joke—the daughter of Dick Valentine, working for truth, justice, and the American way. Her promotion to the Alphas, a nice little house in the suburbs—it was crazy, and she'd been giving serious thought to just blowing out of town, giving the whole thing up, and going back to what she'd been before. . . .

. . . until the two little girls who lived across the street had shown up on her doorstep and asked her with wide, tear-stained eyes if she was really a policeman. Their parents were at work, and they couldn't find their dog. . . .

. . . Becky in her green school dress, little Pris in her overalls—both of them sniffling and shy . . .

The pup had been wandering through a garden only a few blocks away, no sweat—and she'd made two new friends, as easy as that. The sisters had promptly adopted Jill, showing up after school to bring her scraggly bunches of flowers, playing in her yard on weekends, singing her endless songs they'd learned from movies and cartoons. It wasn't like the girls had miraculously changed her outlook or taken away her loneliness—but somehow her thoughts of leaving had been put on a back burner, left alone for awhile. For the first time in her twenty-three years, she'd started to feel like a part of the community she lived and worked in, the change so subtle and gradual that she'd hardly noticed.

Six weeks ago, Becky and Pris had wandered away from a family picnic in Victory Park—and became the first two victims of the psychopaths that had since terrorized the isolated city.

The photo trembled slightly in her hand, sparing her nothing. Becky lying on her back, staring blindly at the sky, a gaping, ragged hole in her belly. Pris was sprawled next to her, arms outstretched, chunks of flesh ripped savagely from the slender limbs. Both children had been eviscerated, dying of massive trauma before they'd bled out. If they'd screamed, no one had heard. . . .

Enough! They're gone, but you can finally do something about it!

Jill fumbled the papers back into their folder, then stepped outside into the early evening, breathing deeply. The scent of freshly cut grass was heavy in the sun-warmed air. Somewhere down the street, a dog barked happily amidst the shouts of children.

She hurried to the small, dented gray hatchback parked by the front walk, forcing herself not to look at the silent McGee house as she started the car and pulled away from the curb. Jill drove through the wide suburban streets of her neighborhood, window down, pushing the speed limit but careful to watch for kids and pets. There weren't many of either around. Since the trouble had started, more and more people were keeping their children and animals indoors, even during the day.

The little hatchback shuddered as she accelerated up the ramp to Highway 202, the warm, dry air whipping her long hair back from her face. It felt good, like waking up from a bad dream. She sped through the sun-dappled evening, the shadows of trees growing long across the road.

Whether it was fate or just the luck of the draw, her life had been touched by what was happening in Raccoon City. She couldn't keep pretending that she was just some jaded ex-thief trying to stay out of jail, trying to toe the line to make her father happy—or that what the S.T.A.R.S. were about to do was just another job. It mattered. It mattered to her that those children were dead, and that the killers were still free to kill again.

The victim files next to her fluttered slightly, the top of the folder caught by the wind; nine restless spirits, perhaps, Becky and Priscilla McGee's among them.

She rested her right hand on the ruffled sheaf,

stilling the gentle movement—and swore to herself that no matter what it took, she was going to find out who was responsible. Whatever she'd been before, whatever she would be in the future, she had changed . . . and wouldn't be able to rest until these murderers of the innocent had been held accountable for their actions.

"Yo, Chris!"

Chris turned away from the soda machine and saw Forest Speyer striding down the empty hall toward him, a wide grin on his tanned, boyish face. Forest was actually a few years older than Chris, but looked like a rebellious teenager—long hair, studded jean jacket, a tattoo of a skull smoking a cigarette on his left shoulder. He was also an excellent mechanic, and one of the best shots Chris had ever seen in action.

"Hey, Forest. What's up?" Chris scooped up a can of club soda from the machine's dispenser and glanced at his watch. He still had a couple of minutes before the meeting. He smiled tiredly as Forest stopped in front of him, blue eyes sparkling. Forest was carrying an armful of equipment—vest, utility belt, and shoulder pack.

"Wesker gave Marini the go-ahead to start the search. Bravo team's goin' in." Even excited, Forest's Alabama twang slowed his words to a stereotypical drawl. He dropped his stuff on one of the visitors' chairs, still grinning widely.

Chris frowned. "When?"

"Now. Soon as I warm up the 'copter." Forest pulled the Kevlar vest on over his T-shirt as he spoke.

"While you Alphas sit taking notes, we're gonna go kick some cannibal *ass!*"

Nothing if not confident, us S.T.A.R.S. "Yeah, well . . . just watch *your* ass, okay? I still think there's more going on here than a couple of slobbering nut jobs hanging around in the woods."

"You know it." Forest pushed his hair back and grabbed his utility belt, obviously already focused on the mission. Chris thought about saying more, but decided against it. For all of his bravado, Forest was a professional; he didn't need to be told to be careful.

You sure about that, Chris? You think Billy was careful enough?

Sighing inwardly, Chris slapped Forest's shoulder lightly and headed for ops through the doorway of the small upstairs waiting room and down the hall. He was surprised that Wesker was sending the teams in separately. Although it was standard for the less experienced S.T.A.R.S. to do the initial recon, this wasn't exactly a standard operation. The number of deaths they were dealing with alone was enough to call for a more aggressive offense. The fact that there were signs of organization to the murders should have brought it to A1 status, and Wesker was still treating it like some kind of a training run.

Nobody else sees it; they didn't know Billy. . . .

Chris thought again about the late-night call he'd gotten last week from his childhood friend. He hadn't heard from Billy in awhile, but knew that he'd taken a research position with Umbrella, the pharmaceutical company that was the single biggest contributor to the economic prosperity of Raccoon City. Billy had never been the type to jump at shadows, and the terrified desperation in his voice had jolted Chris awake, filling him with deep concern. Billy had babbled that his life was in danger, that they were *all* in danger, begged Chris to meet him at a diner at the edge of town—and then never showed up. No one had heard from him since.

Chris had run it over and over again in his mind during the sleepless nights since Billy's disappearance, trying to convince himself that there was no connection to the attacks on Raccoon—and yet was unable to shake his growing certainty that there was more going on than met the eye, and that Billy had known what it was. The cops had checked out Billy's apartment and found nothing to indicate foul play . . . but Chris's instincts told him that his friend was dead, and that he'd been killed by somebody who wanted to keep him from talking.

And I seem to be the only one. Irons doesn't give a shit, and the team thinks I'm just torn up over the loss of an old friend. . . .

He pushed the thoughts aside as he turned the corner, his boot heels sending muted echoes through the arched second floor corridor. He had to focus, to keep his mind on what he *could* do to find out why Billy had disappeared—but he was exhausted, running on a minimum of sleep and an almost constant anxiety that had plagued him since Billy's call. Maybe he *was* losing his perspective, his objectivity dulled by recent events. . . .

He forced himself not to think about anything at all as he neared the S.T.A.R.S. office, determined to be clear-headed for the meeting. The buzzing fluorescents above seemed like overkill in the blazing evening light that filled the tight hallway; the Raccoon police building was a classic, if unconventional, piece of architecture, lots of inlaid tile and heavy wood, but it had too many windows designed to catch the sun. When he'd been a kid, the building had been the Raccoon City Hall. With the population increase a decade back, it had been renovated as a library, and four years ago, turned into a police station. It seemed like there was always some kind of construction going on. . . .

The door to the S.T.A.R.S. office stood open, the muted sounds of gruff male voices spilling out into the hall. Chris hesitated a moment, hearing Chief Irons's among them. "Just call me Brian" Irons was a self-centered and self-serving politician masquerading as a cop. It was no secret that he had his sweaty fingers in more than a few local pies. He'd even been implicated in the Cider district land-scam back in '94, and although nothing had been proved in court, anyone who knew him personally didn't harbor any doubt.

Chris shook his head, listening to Irons's greasy voice. Hard to believe he'd once led the Raccoon S.T.A.R.S., even as a paper-pusher. Maybe even harder to believe that he'd probably end up as mayor someday.

Of course, it doesn't help much that he hates your guts, does it, Redfield?

Yeah, well. Chris didn't like to kiss ass, and Irons didn't know how to have any other kind of relationship. At least Irons wasn't a total incompetent, he'd had some military training. Chris pasted on a straight face and stepped into the small, cluttered office that served as the S.T.A.R.S. filing cabinet and base of operations.

Barry and Joseph were over by the rookie desk, going through a box of papers and talking quietly. Brad Vickers, the Alpha pilot, was drinking coffee and staring at the main computer screen a few feet away, a sour expression on his mild features. Across the room Captain Wesker was leaning back in his chair, hands behind his head, smiling blankly at something Chief Irons was telling him. Irons's bulk was leaned against Wesker's desk, one pudgy hand brushing at his carefully groomed mustache as he spoke.

"So I said, 'You're gonna print what I tell you to print, Bertolucci, and you're gonna *like* it, or you'll never get another quote from this office!' And he says—"

"Chris!" Wesker interrupted the chief, sitting forward. "Good, you're here. Looks like we can stop wasting time."

Irons scowled in his direction but Chris kept his poker face. Wesker didn't care much for Irons, either, and didn't bother trying to be any more than polite in his dealings with the man. From the glint in his eye, it was obvious that he didn't care who knew it, either.

Chris walked into the office and stood by the desk he shared with Ken Sullivan, one of the Bravo team. Since the teams usually worked different shifts, they didn't need much room. He set the unopened can of soda on the battered desktop and looked at Wesker.

"You're sending Bravo in?"

The captain gazed back at him impassively, arms folded across his chest. "Standard procedure, Chris."

Chris sat down, frowning. "Yeah, but with what we talked about last week, I thought—"

Irons interrupted. "I gave the order, Redfield. I know you think that there's some kind of cloak-and-dagger going on here, but *I* don't see any reason to deviate from policy."

Sanctimonious prick. . . .

Chris forced a smile, knowing it would irritate Irons. "Of course, sir. No need to explain yourself on *my* behalf."

Irons glared at him for a moment, his piggy little eyes snapping, then apparently decided to let it drop. He turned back to Wesker. "I'll expect a report when Bravo returns. Now if you'll excuse me, Captain. . . ."

Wesker nodded. "Chief."

Irons stalked past Chris and out of the room. He'd been gone less than a minute before Barry started in.

"Think the chief took a shit today? Maybe we all oughtta chip in for Christmas, get him some laxatives."

Joseph and Brad laughed, but Chris couldn't bring himself to join in. Irons was a joke, but his mishandling of this investigation wasn't all that funny. The S.T.A.R.S. should've been called in at the beginning instead of acting as RPD back up.

He looked back at Wesker, the man's perpetually composed expression hard to read. Wesker had taken over the Raccoon S.T.A.R.S. only a few months ago, transferred by the home office in New York, and Chris still didn't have any real insight into his character. The new captain seemed to be everything he was reputed to be: smooth, professional, cool—but there was a kind of distance to him, a sense that he was often far removed from what was going on. . . .

Wesker sighed and stood up. "Sorry, Chris. I know you wanted things to go different, but Irons didn't put a whole lot of stock into your . . . misgivings."

Chris nodded. Wesker could make recommendations, but Irons was the only one who could upgrade a mission's status. "Not your fault."

Barry walked toward them, scruffing at his short, reddish beard with one giant fist. Barry Burton was only six feet tall but built like a truck. His only passion outside of his family and his weapons collection was weight lifting, and it showed.

"Don't sweat it, Chris. Marini will call us in the second he smells trouble. Irons is just pullin' your chain."

Chris nodded again, but he didn't like it. Hell, Enrico Marini and Forest Speyer were the only experienced soldiers in Bravo. Ken Sullivan was a good scout and a brilliant chemist, but in spite of his S.T.A.R.S. training, he couldn't shoot the broad side of a barn. Richard Aiken was a top-rate communications expert, but he also lacked field experience. Rounding out Bravo team was Rebecca Chambers, who'd only been with the S.T.A.R.S. for three weeks, supposed to be some kind of medical genius. Chris had met her a couple of times and she seemed bright enough, but she was just a kid.

It's not enough. Even with all of us, it may not be enough.

He cracked open his soda but didn't drink any, wondering instead what the S.T.A.R.S. were going up against, Billy's pleading, desperate words echoing through his mind yet again.

"They're going to kill me, Chris! They're going to kill everyone who knows! Meet me at Emmy's, now, I'll tell you everything. . . ."

Exhausted, Chris stared off into space, alone in the knowledge that the savage murders were only the tip of the proverbial iceberg.

Barry stood by Chris's desk for a minute, trying to think of something else to say, but Chris didn't look like he was in the mood for conversation. Barry shrugged inwardly and headed back to where Joseph was going through files. Chris was a good guy, but he took things too hard sometimes; he'd get over it as soon as it was their turn to step in.

Man, it was hot! Seemingly endless trickles of sweat rolled down his spine, gluing his T-shirt to his broad back. The air-conditioning was on the fritz as usual, and even with the door open, the tiny S.T.A.R.S. office was uncomfortably warm.

"Any luck?"

Joseph looked up at him from the pile of papers, a rueful smirk on his lean face. "You kidding? It's like somebody hid the damn thing on purpose."

Barry sighed and scooped up a handful of files. "Maybe Jill found it. She was still here when I left last night, going through the witness reports for about the hundredth time. . . ."

"What are you two looking for, anyway?" Brad asked.

Barry and Joseph both looked over at Brad, still sitting at the computer console, headset on. He'd be monitoring Bravo's progress throughout their fly-by of the forested district, but for now he looked bored as hell.

Joseph answered him. "Ah, Barry claims that there are floor plans in here somewhere on the old Spencer estate, some architectural digest that came out when the house was built—" He paused, then grinned at Brad. "Except that I'm thinkin' that ol' Barry's gone senile on us. They say memory is the first thing to go."

Barry scowled good-naturedly. "Ol' Barry could easily kick your ass into next week, little man."

Joseph looked at him mock-seriously. "Yeah, but would you *remember* it afterwards?"

Barry chuckled, shaking his head. He was only thirty-eight, but had been with the Raccoon S.T.A.R.S. for fifteen years, making him the senior member. He endured numerous old age jokes, mostly from Joseph.

Brad cocked an eyebrow. "The Spencer place? Why would it be in a magazine?"

"You kids, gotta learn your history," Barry said. "It was designed by the one and only George Trevor, just before he disappeared. He was that hot-shit architect who did all those weird skyscrapers in D.C.—in fact, Trevor's disappearance may have been the reason that Spencer shut the mansion down. Rumor has it that

Trevor went crazy during the construction and when it was finished, he got lost and wandered the halls until he starved to death."

Brad scoffed, but suddenly looked uneasy. "That's bullshit. I never heard anything like that."

Joseph winked at Barry. "No, it's true. Now his tortured ghost roams the estate each night, pale and emaciated, and I've heard tell that sometimes you can hear him, calling out, 'Brad Vickers . . . bring me Brad Vickers. . . .'"

Brad flushed slightly. "Yeah, ha ha. You're a real comedian, Frost."

Barry shook his head, smiling, but wondered again how Brad had ever made it to Alpha. He was undoubtedly the best hacker working for S.T.A.R.S., and a decent enough pilot, but he wasn't so hot under pressure. Joseph had taken to calling him "Chickenheart Vickers" when he wasn't around, and while the S.T.A.R.S. generally stuck up for one another, nobody disagreed with Joseph's assessment.

"So *is* that why Spencer shut it down?" Brad addressed this to Barry, his cheeks still red.

Barry shrugged. "I doubt it. It was supposed to be some kind of guest house for Umbrella's top execs. Trevor *did* disappear right about the time of completion—but Spencer was whacko, anyway. He decided to move Umbrella's headquarters to Europe, I forget where exactly, and just boarded up the mansion. Probably a couple million bucks, straight into the crapper."

Joseph sneered. "Right. Like Umbrella would suffer."

True enough. Spencer may have been crazy, but he'd had enough money and business savvy to hire the right people. Umbrella was one of the biggest medical research and pharmaceutical companies on the planet. Even thirty years ago, the loss of a few million dollars probably hadn't hurt.

"Anyway," Joseph went on, "the Umbrella people told Irons that they'd sent someone out to check the place over, and that it was secure, no break-ins."

"So why look for blueprints?" Brad asked.

It was Chris who answered, startling Barry. He'd walked back to join them, his youthful face fixed with a sudden intensity that almost bordered on obsessive. "Because it's the only place in the woods that hasn't been checked over by the police, and it's practically in the middle of the crime scenes. And because you can't always trust what people say."

Brad frowned. "But if Umbrella sent somebody out . . ."

Whatever Chris was going to say in response was cut short by Wesker's smooth voice, rising from the front of the room.

"All right, people. Since it appears that Ms. Valentine isn't planning on joining us, why don't we get this started?"

Barry walked to his desk, worried about Chris for the first time since this whole thing had started. He'd recruited the younger man for the S.T.A.R.S. a few years back thanks to a chance encounter in a local gun shop. Chris had proved to be an asset to the team, bright and thoughtful as well as a top-notch marksman and able pilot.

But now . . .

Barry gazed fondly at the picture of Kathy and the girls that sat on his desk. Chris's obsession with the murders in Raccoon was understandable, particularly since his friend had disappeared. Nobody in town wanted to see another life lost. Barry had a family, and was as determined as anyone else on the team to stop the killers. But Chris's relentless suspicion had gone a little overboard. What had he meant by that, "you can't always trust what people say"? Either that Umbrella was lying or Chief Irons was. . . .

Ridiculous. Umbrella's branch chemical plant and administrative buildings on the outskirts of town supplied three-quarters of the jobs in Raccoon City; it would be counter-productive for them to lie. Besides, Umbrella's integrity was at least as solid as any other major corporation's—maybe some industrial espionage, but medical secret-swapping was a far cry from murder. And Chief Irons, though a fat, weasely blowhard, wasn't the kind to get his hands any dirtier than they'd get accepting illegal campaign funds; the guy wanted to be *mayor,* for chrissake.

Barry's gaze lingered on the picture of his family a moment longer before he turned his chair around to face Wesker's desk, and he suddenly realized that he wanted Chris to be wrong. Whatever was going on in Raccoon City, that kind of vicious brutality couldn't be planned. And that meant . . .

Barry didn't know what that meant. He sighed, and waited for the meeting to begin.

†wo

JILL WAS DEEPLY RELIEVED TO HEAR THE
sound of Wesker's voice as she jogged toward the
open door of the S.T.A.R.S. office. She'd seen one of
their helicopters taking off as she'd arrived, and been
positive that they'd left without her. The S.T.A.R.S.
were a fairly casual outfit in some respects. But there
also wasn't any room for people who couldn't keep
up—and she wanted very much to be in on this case
from the beginning.

"The RPD has already established a perimeter
search, spanning sectors one, four, seven, and nine.
It's the central zones we're concerned with, and Bravo
will set down *here* . . ."

At least she wasn't *too* late; Wesker always ran
meetings the same way—update speech, theory, then

Q and A. Jill took a deep breath and stepped into the office. Wesker was pointing to a posted map at the front of the room, dotted with colored tags where the bodies had been found. He hardly faltered in his speech as she walked quickly to her desk, feeling suddenly like she was back in basic training and had shown up late for class.

Chris Redfield threw her a half-smile as she sat down, and she nodded back at him before focusing on Wesker. She didn't know any of the Raccoon team that well, but Chris had made a real effort to make her feel welcome since she'd arrived.

". . . after a fly-by of the other central areas. Once they report in, we'll have a better idea of where to focus our energies."

"But what about the Spencer place?" Chris asked. "It's practically in the middle of the crime scenes. If we start there, we can conduct a more complete search—"

"—and if Bravo's information points to that area, rest assured, we'll search there. For now, I don't see any reason to consider it a priority."

Chris looked incredulous. "But we only have Umbrella's word that the estate is secure. . . ."

Wesker leaned against his desk, his strong features expressionless. "Chris, we all want to get to the bottom of this. But we have to work as a team, and the best approach here is to do a thorough search for those missing hikers before we start jumping to conclusions. Bravo will take a look-see and we'll conduct this by the book."

Chris frowned, but said nothing more. Jill resisted

the urge to roll her eyes at Wesker's little speech. He was doing the right thing, technically, but had left out the part about it being politic to do as Chief Irons wanted. Irons had made it clear time and again throughout the killing spree that he was in charge of the investigation and was calling the shots. It wouldn't have bothered her so much except that Wesker presented himself as an independent thinker, a man who didn't play politics. She had joined the S.T.A.R.S. because she couldn't stand the bullshit red-tape that dominated so much of law enforcement, and Wesker's obvious deferral to the chief was irritating.

Well, and don't forget that you stood a good chance of ending up in prison if you hadn't changed your occupation. . . .

"Jill. I see that you managed to find the time to come in. Illuminate us with your brilliant insight. What have you got for us?"

Jill met Wesker's sharp gaze evenly, trying to seem as cool and composed as he was. "Nothing new, I'm afraid. The only obvious pattern is location. . . ."

She looked down at the notes she had on the stack of files in front of her, scanning them for reference. "Uh, the tissue samples from underneath both Becky McGee's and Chris Smith's fingernails were an exact match, we got that yesterday . . . and Tonya Lipton, the third victim, had definitely been hiking in the foothills, that'd be sector—seven-B. . . ."

She looked back up at Wesker and made her pitch. "My theory at this point is that there's a possible ritualistic cult hiding in the mountains, four to eleven members strong, with guard dogs trained to attack intruders in their territory."

"Extrapolate." Wesker folded his arms, waiting.

At least no one had laughed. Jill plunged forward, warming to the material. "The cannibalism and dismemberment suggest ritualistic behavior, as does the presence of decomposed flesh found on some of the victims—like the killers are carrying parts of previous unknown victims to their attacks. We've got saliva and tissue samples from four separate human assailants, though eye-witness reports suggest up to ten or eleven people. And those killed by animals were all found or found to be attacked in the same vicinity, suggesting that they wandered into some kind of off-limits area. The saliva traces appear to be canine, though there's still some disagreement. . . ." She trailed off, finished.

Wesker's face betrayed nothing, but he nodded slowly. "Not bad, not bad at all. Disprove?"

Jill sighed. She hated having to shoot her own theory down, but that was part of the job—and in all honesty, the part that most encouraged clear, rational thinking. The S.T.A.R.S. trained their people not to fixate on any single path to the truth.

She glanced at her notes again. "It's highly unlikely that a cult that big would move around much, and the murders started too recently to be local; the RPD would've seen signs before now, some escalation to this kind of behavior. Also, the level of post-mortem violence indicates disorganized offenders, and they usually work solo."

Joseph Frost, the Alpha vehicle specialist, piped up

from the back of the room. "The animal attack part works, though, protecting their territory and all that."

Wesker scooped up a pen and walked to the dry-erase board next to his desk, talking as he moved. "I agree."

He wrote *territoriality* on the board and then turned back to face her. "Anything else?"

Jill shook her head, but felt good that she'd contributed something. She knew the cult aspect was reaching, but it had been all she could come up with. The police certainly hadn't come up with anything better.

Wesker turned his attention to Brad Vickers, who suggested that it was a new strain of terrorism, and that demands would be made soon. Wesker put *terrorism* on the board, but didn't seem enthusiastic about the idea. Neither did anyone else. Brad quickly went back to his headset, checking on Bravo team's status.

Both Joseph and Barry passed on theorizing, and Chris's views on the killings were already well known, if vague; he believed that there was an organized assault going on, and that external influences were involved somehow. Wesker asked if he had anything new to add (stressing *new,* Jill noticed), and Chris shook his head, looking depressed.

Wesker capped the black pen and sat on the edge of his desk, gazing thoughtfully at the blank expanse of board. "It's a start," he said. "I know you've all read the police and coroner reports, and listened to the eyewitness accounts—"

"Vickers here, over." From the back of the room, Brad spoke quietly into his headset, interrupting Wesker. The captain lowered his voice and continued.

"Now at this point, we don't know what we're dealing with and I know that all of us have some . . . *concerns* with how the RPD has been dealing with the situation. But now that we're on the case, I—"

"*What?*"

At the sound of Brad's raised voice, Jill turned toward the back of the room along with everyone else. He was standing up, agitated, one hand pressed to the ear piece of his set.

"Bravo team, report. Repeat, Bravo team, report!"

Wesker stood up. "Vickers, put it on 'com!"

Brad hit the switch on his console and the bright, crackling sound of static filled the room. Jill strained to hear a human voice amidst the fuzz, but for several tense seconds, there was nothing.

Then. "*. . . you copy? Malfunction, we're going to have to . . .*"

The rest was lost in a burst of static. It sounded like Enrico Marini, the Bravo team leader. Jill chewed at her lower lip and exchanged a worried glance with Chris. Enrico had seemed . . . frantic. They all listened for another moment but there was nothing more than the sound of open air.

"Position?" Wesker snapped.

Brad's face was pale. "They're in the, uh, sector twenty-two, tail end of C . . . except I've lost the signal. The transmitter is off-line."

Jill felt stunned, saw the feeling reflected in the faces of the others. The helicopter's transmitter was designed to keep working no matter what; the only way it would shut down was if something big happened—the entire system blanking out or being seriously damaged.

Something like a crash.

Chris felt his stomach knot as he recognized the coordinates.

The Spencer estate.

Marini had said something about a malfunction, it had to be a coincidence—but it didn't *feel* like one. The Bravos were in trouble, and practically on top of the old Umbrella mansion.

All of this went through his head in a split-second, and then he was standing, ready to move. Whatever happened, the S.T.A.R.S. took care of their own.

Wesker was already in action. He addressed the team even as he reached for his keys, heading for the gun safe.

"Joseph, take over the board and keep trying to raise them. Vickers, warm up the 'copter and get clearance, I want us ready to fly in five."

The captain unlocked the safe as Brad handed the headset to Joseph and hurried out of the room. The reinforced metal door swung open, revealing an arsenal of rifles and handguns shelved above boxes of ammo. Wesker turned to the rest of them, his expression as bland as ever but his voice brisk with authority.

"Barry, Chris—I want you to get the weapons into the 'copter, loaded and secured. Jill, get the vests and packs and meet us on the roof." He clipped a key off his ring and tossed it to her.

"I'm going to put a call in to Irons, make sure he

gets us some backup and EMTs down at the barricade," Wesker said, then blew out sharply. "Five minutes or less, folks. Let's move."

Jill left for the locker room and Barry grabbed one of the empty duffel bags from the bottom of the gun safe, nodding at Chris. Chris scooped up a second bag and started loading boxes of shells, cartridges, and clips as Barry carefully handled the weapons, checking each one. Behind them, Joseph again tried hailing the Bravo team to no avail.

Chris wondered again about the proximity of the Bravo team's last reported position to the Spencer estate. Was there a connection? And if so, how?

Billy worked for Umbrella, they own the estate—

"Chief? Wesker. We just lost contact with Bravo; I'm taking us in."

Chris felt a sudden rush of adrenaline and worked faster, aware that every second counted—could mean the difference between life and death for his friends and teammates. A serious crash was unlikely, the Bravos would have been flying low and Forest was a decent pilot . . . but what about after they'd gone down?

Wesker quickly relayed the information to Irons over the phone and then hung up, walking back to join them.

"I'm going up to make sure our 'copter's outfitted. Joseph, give it another minute and then turn it over to the boys at the front desk. You can help these two carry the equipment up. I'll see you on top."

Wesker nodded to them and hurried out, his footsteps clattering loudly down the hall.

"He's good," Barry said quietly, and Chris had to agree. It was reassuring to see that their new captain didn't rattle easily. Chris still wasn't sure how he felt about the man personally, but his respect for Wesker's abilities was growing by the minute.

"Come in, Bravo, do you copy? Repeat . . ."

Joseph patiently went on, his voice tight with strain, his pleas lost to the haze of white static that pulsed out into the room.

Wesker strode down the deserted hall and through the shabbier of the two second-floor waiting rooms, nodding briskly at a pair of uniforms that stood talking by the soda machine.

The door to the outside landing was chocked open, a faint, humid breeze cutting through the stickiness of the air inside. It was still daylight, but not for much longer. He hoped that wouldn't complicate matters, although he figured it probably would. . . .

Wesker took a left and started down the winding corridor that led to the helipad, absently running through a mental checklist.

. . . *hailing open procedure, weapons, gear, report . . .*

He already knew that everything was in order, but went through it again anyway; it didn't pay to get sloppy, and assumptions were the first step down that path. He liked to think of himself as a man of precision, one who had taken all possibilities into account and decided on the best course of action after thoroughly weighing all factors. Control was what being a competent leader was all about.

But to close this case—

He shut the thought down before it could get any further. He knew what had to be done, and there was still plenty of time. All he needed to concentrate on now was getting the Bravos back, safe and sound.

Wesker opened the door at the end of the hall and stepped out into the bright evening, the rising hum of the 'copter's engine and the smell of machine oil filling his senses. The small rooftop helipad was cooler than inside, partly draped by the shadow of an aging water tower, and empty except for the gunmetal gray Alpha helicopter. For the first time, he wondered what had gone wrong for Bravo; he'd had Joseph and the rookie check both birds out yesterday and they'd been fine, all systems go.

He dismissed *that* train of thought as he walked toward the 'copter, his shadow falling long across the concrete. It didn't matter why, not anymore. What mattered was what came next. *Expect the unexpected,* that was the S.T.A.R.S. motto—although that basically meant to prepare for anything.

Expect nothing, that was Albert Wesker's motto. A little less catchy, maybe, but infinitely more useful. It virtually guaranteed that nothing would ever surprise him.

He stepped up to the open pilot door and got a shaky thumbs-up from Vickers; the man looked positively green, and Wesker briefly considered leaving him behind. Chris was licensed to fly, and Vickers had a reputation for choking under the gun; the last thing he needed was for one of his people to freeze up if there was trouble. Then he thought about the lost

Bravos and decided against it. This was a rescue mission. The worst Vickers could do would be to throw up on himself if the 'copter had crashed badly, and Wesker could live with that.

He opened the side door and crouched his way into the cabin, doing a quick inventory of the equipment that lined the walls. Emergency flares, ration kits . . . he popped the lid on the heavy, dented footlocker behind the benches and looked through the basic medical supplies, nodding to himself. They were as ready as they were going to be . . .

Wesker grinned suddenly, wondering what Brian Irons was doing right now.

Shitting his pants, no doubt. Wesker chuckled as he stepped back out onto the sun-baked asphalt, getting a sudden clear mental image of Irons, his pudgy cheeks red with anger and crap dribbling down his leg. Irons liked to think he could control everything and everyone around him and lost his temper when he couldn't, and that made him an idiot.

Unfortunately for all of them, he was an idiot with a little bit of power. Wesker had checked him out carefully before taking the position in Raccoon City, and knew a few things about the chief that didn't paint him in a particularly positive light. He had no intention of using that information, but if Irons attempted to screw things up one more time, Wesker had no qualms about letting that information get out. . . .

. . . or at least telling him that I have access to it; it'd certainly keep him out of the way.

Barry Burton stepped out onto the concrete carrying the ammo cache, his giant biceps flexing as he shifted his hold on the heavy canvas bag and started for the 'copter. Chris and Joseph followed, Chris with the sidearms and Joseph lugging a satchel of RPGs, the compact grenade launcher slung over one shoulder.

Wesker marveled at Burton's brute strength as the Alpha climbed in and casually set the bag down as though it didn't weigh over a hundred pounds. Barry was bright enough, but in the S.T.A.R.S., muscle was a definite asset. Everyone else in his squad was in good shape, but compared to Barry, they were pencil-necks.

As the three of them stored the equipment, Wesker turned his attention back to the door, watching for Jill. He checked his watch and frowned. It had been just under five minutes since their last contact with Bravo, they'd made excellent time . . . so where the hell was Valentine? He hadn't interacted with her much since she'd come to Raccoon, but her file was a rave review. She'd gotten high recommendations from everyone she'd worked with, praised by her last captain as highly intelligent and "unusually" calm in a crisis. She'd have to be, with her history. Her father was Dick Valentine, the best thief in the business a couple of decades back. He'd trained her to follow in his footsteps, and word had it that she had done quite well until Daddy had been incarcerated. . . .

Prodigy or no, she could stand to buy a decent watch. He silently urged Jill to get her ass into gear and motioned for Vickers to start the blades turning.

It was time to find out how bad things were out there.

THREE

JILL TURNED TOWARD THE DOOR OF THE
dim and silent S.T.A.R.S. locker room, her arms full
with two bulging duffel bags. She set them down and
quickly pulled her hair back, tucking it into a well-
worn black beret. It was really too hot, but it was her
lucky hat. She glanced at her watch before hefting the
bags, pleased to note that it had only taken her three
minutes to load up.

She'd gone through all of the Alpha lockers, grabbing utility belts, fingerless gloves, Kevlar vests and
shoulder packs, noting that the lockers reflected their
user's personalities: Barry's had been covered with
snapshots of his family and a pin-up from a gun
magazine, a rare .45 Luger, shining against red velvet.
Chris had pictures of his Air Force buddies up and the
shelves were a boyish mess—crumpled T-shirts, loose

papers, even a glow-in-the-dark yo-yo with a broken string. Brad Vickers had a stack of self-help books and Joseph, a Three Stooges calendar. Only Wesker's had been devoid of personal effects. Somehow, it didn't surprise her. The captain struck her as too tightly wound to place much value on sentiment.

Her own locker held a number of used paperback true crime novels, a toothbrush, floss, breath mints, and three hats. On the door was a small mirror and an old, frayed photo of her and her father, taken when she was a child and they'd gone to the beach one summer. As she'd quickly thrown the Alpha gear together, she decided that she'd redecorate when she had free time; anyone looking through her locker would think she was some kind of dental freak.

Jill crouched a bit and fumbled at the latch to the door, balancing the awkward bags on one raised knee. She'd just grasped it when someone coughed loudly behind her.

Startled, Jill dropped the bags and spun, looking for the cougher as her mind reflexively assessed the situation. The door had been locked. The small room held three banks of lockers and had been quiet and dark when she'd come in. There was another door in the back of the room, but no one had come through it since she'd entered—

—which means that someone was already here when I came in, in the shadows behind the last bank. A cop grabbing a nap?

Unlikely. The department's lunch room had a couple of bunks in the back, a lot more comfortable than a narrow bench over cold concrete.

*Then maybe it's someone enjoying a little "leisure"
time with a magazine,* her brain snarled, *does it
matter? You're on the clock here, get moving!*

Right. Jill scooped up the bags and turned to leave.

"Miss Valentine, isn't it?" A shadow separated
itself from the back of the room and stepped forward,
a tall man with a low, musical voice. Early forties, a
thin frame, dark hair and deep set eyes. He was
actually wearing a trench coat, and an expensive one
at that.

Jill readied herself to move quickly if the need
arose. She didn't recognize him.

"That's right," she said warily.

The man stepped toward her, a smile flickering
across his face. "I have something for you," he said
softly.

Jill narrowed her eyes and shifted automatically
into a defensive position, balancing her weight on the
balls of her feet. "Hold it, asshole—I don't know who
the hell you think you are or what you think I want,
but you're in a police station . . ."

She trailed off as he shook his head, grinning
broadly, his dark eyes twinkling with mirth. "You
mistake my intentions, Miss Valentine. Excuse my
manners, please. My name is Trent, and I'm . . . a
friend to the S.T.A.R.S."

Jill studied his posture and position and eased her
own stance slightly, watching his eyes for even a
flicker of movement. She didn't feel threatened by
him, exactly. . . .

. . . but how did he know my name?

"What do you want?"

Trent grinned wider. "Ah, straight to the point. But of course, you're on a rather tight schedule. . . ."

He slowly reached into a pocket of his coat and pulled out what looked like a cell phone. "Though it's not what *I* want that's important. It's what I think you should have."

Jill glanced quickly at the item he held, frowning. "That?"

"Yes. I've assembled a few documents that you should find interesting; compelling, in fact." As he spoke, he held out the device.

She reached for it carefully, realizing as she did that it was a mini-disk reader, a very complicated and costly micro computer. Trent was well-financed, whoever he was.

Jill tucked the reader into her hip pack, suddenly more than a little curious. "Who do you work for?"

He shook his head. "That's not important, not at this juncture. Although I will say that there are a lot of very important people watching Raccoon City right now."

"Oh? And are these people 'friends' of the S.T.A.R.S., too, Mr. Trent?"

Trent laughed, a soft, deep chuckle. "So many questions, so little time. Read the files. And if I were you, I wouldn't mention this conversation to anyone; it could have rather serious consequences."

He walked toward the door in the back of the room, turning back to her as he reached for the knob. Trent's lined, weathered features suddenly lost all trace of humor, his gaze serious and intense.

"One more thing, Miss Valentine, and this is critical, make no mistake: not everyone can be trusted, and not everyone is who they appear to be—even the people you think you know. If you want to stay alive, you'll do well to remember it."

Trent opened the door and just like that, he was gone.

Jill stared after him, her mind going a million directions at once. She felt like she was in some melodramatic old spy movie and had just met the mysterious stranger. It was laughable, and yet—

—*and yet he just handed you several thousands of dollars worth of equipment with a straight face and told you to watch your back; you think he's kidding?*

She didn't know what to think, and she didn't have time to think it; the Alpha team was probably assembled, waiting, and wondering where the hell she was.

Jill shouldered the heavy bags and hurried out the door.

They'd gotten the weapons loaded and secured and Wesker was getting impatient. Although his eyes were hidden by dark aviator sunglasses, Chris could see it in the captain's stance and in the way he kept his head cocked toward the building. The helicopter was prepped and ready, the blades whipping warm, humid air through the tight compartment. With the door open, the sound of the engine drowned out any attempt at conversation. There was nothing to do but wait.

Come on, Jill, don't slow us up here. . . .

Even as Chris thought it, Jill emerged from the building and jogged toward them with the Alpha gear, an apologetic look on her face. Wesker jumped down to help her, taking one of the stuffed bags as she climbed aboard.

Wesker followed, closing the double hatches behind them. Instantly, the roar of the turbine engine was muted to a dull thrum.

"Problems, Jill?" Wesker didn't sound angry, but there was an edge to his voice that suggested he wasn't all that happy, either.

Jill shook her head. "One of the lockers was stuck. I had a hell of a time getting the key to work."

The captain stared at her for a moment, as if deciding whether or not to give her a hard time, then shrugged. "I'll call maintenance when we get back. Go ahead and distribute the gear."

He picked up a headset and put it on, moving up to sit next to Brad as Jill started passing out the vests. The helicopter lifted slowly, the RPD building falling away as Brad positioned them to head northwest.

Chris crouched down next to Jill after donning his vest, helping her sort through the gloves and belts as they sped over the city toward the Arklay Mountains. The busy urban streets below quickly gave way to the suburbs, wide streets and quiet houses set amidst squares of browning grass and picket fences. An evening haze had settled over the sprawling but isolated community, fuzzing the edges of the picturesque view and giving it an unreal, dream-like quality. Minutes passed in silence as the Alphas prepared themselves and belted in, each team member preoccupied with his or her own thoughts.

With any luck, the Bravo team's helicopter had

suffered only a minor mechanical failure. Forest would've set it down in one of the scraggly open fields that dotted the forest and was probably up to his elbows in grease by now, cursing at the engine as they waited for Alpha to show. Without the bird in working order, Marini wouldn't start the proposed search. The alternative . . .

Chris grimaced, not wanting to consider any alternatives. He'd once seen the aftermath of a serious 'copter crash, back in the Air Force. Pilot error had led to the fall of a Huey carrying eleven men and women to a training mission. By the time the rescuers had arrived, there'd been nothing but charred, smoking bones amidst the fiery debris, the sweet, sticky smell of gasoline-roasted flesh heavy in the blackened air. Even the ground had been burning, and that was the image that had haunted his dreams for months afterwards; the earth on fire, the chemical flames devouring the very soil beneath his feet. . . .

There was a slight dip in their altitude as Brad adjusted the rotor pitch, jolting him out of the unpleasant memory. The ragged outskirts of Raccoon Forest slipped by below, the orange markers of the police blockade standing out against the thick muted green of the trees. Twilight was finally setting in, the forest growing heavy with shadow.

"ETA . . . three minutes," Brad called back, and Chris looked around the cabin, noting the silent, grim expressions of his teammates. Joseph had tied a bandana over his head and was intently relacing his boots. Barry was gently rubbing a soft cloth over his beloved Colt Python, staring out the hatch window.

He turned his head to look at Jill and was surprised to find her staring back at him thoughtfully. She was sitting on the same bench as him and she smiled briefly, almost nervously as he caught her gaze. Abruptly she unhooked her belt and moved to sit next to him. He caught a faint scent of her skin, a clean, soapy smell.

"Chris . . . what you've been saying, about external factors in these cases . . ."

Her voice was pitched so low that he had to lean in to hear her over the throbbing of the engine. She glanced quickly around at the others, as if to make sure that no one was listening, then looked into his eyes, her own carefully guarded.

"I think you might be on the right track," she said softly, "and I'm starting to think that it might not be such a good idea to talk about it."

Chris's throat suddenly felt dry. "Did something happen?"

Jill shook her head, her finely chiseled features giving away nothing. "No. I've just been thinking that maybe you should watch what you say. Maybe not everyone listening is on the right side of this. . . ."

Chris frowned, not sure what she was trying to tell him. "The only people I've talked to are on the job—"

Her gaze didn't falter, and he realized suddenly what she was implying.

Jesus, and I thought I was paranoid!

"Jill, I *know* these people, and even if I didn't, the S.T.A.R.S. have psych profiles on every member, history checks, personal references—there's no way it could happen."

She sighed. "Look, forget I said anything. I just . . . just watch yourself, that's all."

"All right, kids, look lively! We're coming up on sector twenty-two, they could be anywhere."

At Wesker's interruption, Jill gave him a final sharp glance and then moved to one of the windows. Chris followed, Joseph and Barry taking the search up on the other side of the cabin.

Looking out the small window, he scanned the deepening dusk on automatic, thinking about what Jill had said. He supposed he should be grateful that he wasn't the only one who suspected some kind of a cover up—but why hadn't she said anything before? And to warn him against the S.T.A.R.S. . . .

She knows something.

She must, it was the only explanation that made any sense. He decided that after they picked up Bravo, he'd talk to her again, try to convince her that going to Wesker would be their best bet. With both of them pushing, the captain would have to listen.

He stared out at the seemingly endless sea of trees as the helicopter skimmed lower, forcing his full attention to the search. The Spencer estate had to be close, though he couldn't see it in the fading light. Thoughts of Billy and Umbrella and now Jill's strange warning circled through his exhaustion, trying to break his focus, but he refused to give in. He was still worried about the Bravos—though as the trees swept by, he was becoming more and more convinced that they weren't in any real trouble. It was probably nothing worse than a crossed wire, Forest had just shut it down to make repairs—

Then he saw it less than a mile away, even as Jill pointed and spoke, and his concern turned to cold dread.

"Look, Chris—"

An oily plume of black smoke boiled up through the last remnants of daylight, staining the sky like a promise of death.

Oh, no—

Barry clenched his jaw, staring at the stream of smoke that rose up from the trees, feeling sick.

"Captain, two o'clock sharp!" Chris called, and then they were turning, heading for the dark smudge that could only mean a crash.

Wesker moved back into the cabin, still wearing his shades. He stepped to the window and spoke quietly, his voice subdued. "Let's not assume the worst. There's a possibility that a fire broke out after they landed, or that they started the fire on purpose, as a signal—"

Barry wished they could believe him, but even Wesker had to know better. With the 'copter shut down, a fire starting on its own was unlikely—and if the Bravos wanted to signal, they would've used flares.

Besides which, wood doesn't make that kind of smoke. . . .

"—but whatever it is, we won't know till we get there. Now if I could have your full attention, please."

Barry turned away from the window, saw the others do the same. Chris, Jill, and Joseph all wore the same look, as he imagined he did: shock. S.T.A.R.S. some-

43

times got hurt in the line of duty, it was part of the job—but accidents like this . . .

Wesker's only visible sign of distress was the set of his mouth, a thin, grim line against his tanned skin. "Listen up. We've got people down in a possibly hostile environment. I want all of you armed, and I want an organized approach, a standard fan as soon as we set down. Barry, you'll take point."

Barry nodded, pulling himself together. Wesker was right; now was not the time to get emotional.

"Brad's going to set us down as close to the site as he can get, what looks like a small clearing about fifty meters south of their last coordinates. He'll stay with the 'copter and keep it warm in case of trouble. Any questions?"

Nobody spoke, and Wesker nodded briskly. "Good. Barry, load us up. We can leave the rest of the gear on board and come back for it."

The captain stepped to the front to talk to Brad, while Jill, Chris, and Joseph turned to Barry. As weapons specialist, he checked the firearms in and out to each S.T.A.R.S. team member and kept them in prime condition.

Barry turned to the cabinet next to the outer hatch and unhooked the latch, exposing six Beretta 9mm handguns on a metal rack, cleaned and sighted only yesterday. Each weapon held fifteen rounds, semi-jacketed hollow points. It was a good gun, though Barry preferred his Python, a lot bigger punch with .357 rounds. . . .

He quickly distributed the weapons, passing out three loaded clips with each.

"I hope we don't need these," Joseph said, slapping in a clip, and Barry nodded agreement. Just because he paid his dues to the NRA didn't mean he was some trigger-happy dumbass, looking to kill; he just liked guns.

Wesker joined them again and the five of them stood at the hatch, waiting for Brad to bring them in. As they neared the plume of smoke, the helicopter's whirling blades pushed it down and out, creating a black fog that blended into the heavy shadows of the trees. Any chance of spotting the downed vehicle from the air was lost to the smoke and dusk.

Brad swung them around and settled the bird into a scrappy patch of tall grass, snapping wildly from the forced wind. Even as the rails wobbled to the ground, Barry had his hand on the latch, ready to move out.

A warm hand fell on his shoulder. Barry turned and saw Chris looking at him intently.

"We're right behind you," Chris said, and Barry nodded. He wasn't worried, not with the Alphas backing him up. All he was concerned with was the Bravo team's situation. Rico Marini was a good friend of his. Marini's wife had baby-sat for the girls more times than Barry could count, and was friends with Kathy. The thought of him dead, to a stupid mechanical screw-up . . .

Hang on, buddy, we're comin'.

One hand on the butt of his Colt, Barry pulled the handle and stepped out into the humid, whipping twilight of Raccoon Forest, ready for anything.

FOUR

THEY SPREAD OUT AND STARTED NORTH,
Wesker and Chris behind and to Barry's left, Jill and
Joseph on his right. Directly in front of them was a
sparse stand of trees, and as the Alpha's 'copter blade
revved down, Jill could smell burning fuel and see
wisps of smoke curling through the foliage.

They moved quickly through the wooded area,
visibility dropping off sharply beneath the needled
branches. The warm scents of pine and earth were
overshadowed by the burning smell, the acrid odor
growing stronger with each step. From the dim light
filtering toward them, Jill saw that there was another
clearing ahead, high with brittle grasses.

"I see it, dead ahead!"

Jill felt her heart speed up at Barry's shout, and

then they were all running, hurrying to catch up to their point man.

She emerged from the copse of trees, Joseph next to her. Barry was already at the downed 'copter, Chris and Wesker right behind. Smoke was still rising from the silent wreck, but it was thinning. If there had been a fire, it had died out.

She and Joseph reached the others and stopped, staring, no one speaking as they surveyed the scene. The long, wide body of the 'copter was intact, not a single scratch visible. The port landing rail looked bent, but besides that and the dying haze of smoke from the rotor, there seemed to be nothing wrong with it. The hatches stood open, the beam from Wesker's penlight showing them an undamaged cabin. From what she could see, most of the Bravo's gear was still on board.

So where are they?

It didn't make any sense. It hadn't been fifteen minutes since their last transmission; if anyone had been injured, they would have stayed. And if they'd decided to leave, why had they left their equipment behind?

Wesker handed the light to Joseph and nodded toward the cockpit. "Check it out. The rest of you, spread out, look for clues—tracks, shell casings, signs of struggle—you find anything, let me know. And stay alert."

Jill stood a moment longer, staring at the smoking 'copter and wondering what could have happened. Enrico had said something about a malfunction; so okay, the Bravos had set down. What had happened next? What would have made them abandon their best chance of being found, leaving behind emergency kits, weaponry—Jill saw a couple of bullet-proof vests crumpled next to the hatch and shook her head, adding it to the growing list of seemingly irrational actions.

She turned to join the search as Joseph stepped out of the cockpit, looking as confused as she felt. She waited to hear his report as he handed the light back to Wesker, shrugging nervously.

"I don't know what happened. The bent rail suggests a forced landing, but except for the electrical system, everything looks fine."

Wesker sighed, then raised his voice so the others could hear. "Circle out, people, three meters apart, widen as we go!"

Jill moved over to stand between Chris and Barry, both men already scanning the ground at their feet as they slowly moved east and northeast of the helicopter. Wesker stepped into the cabin, probing the darkness with his penlight. Joseph headed west.

Dry weeds crackled underfoot as they widened their circle, the only sound in the still, warm air except for the distant hum of the Alpha helicopter engine. Jill used her boots to search through the thick ground cover, brushing the tall grasses aside with each step. In another few moments, it'd be too dark to see anything; they needed to break out the flashlights, Bravo had left theirs behind. . . .

Jill stopped suddenly, listening. The sighing, crackling steps of the others, the far away drone of their 'copter—

—and nothing else. Not a chirp, a chitter, nothing.

They were in the woods, in the middle of summer; where were the animals, the insects? The forest was unnaturally still, the only sounds human. For the first time since they'd set down, Jill was afraid.

She was about to call out to the others when Joseph shouted from somewhere behind them, his voice high and cracking.

"Hey! Over here!"

Jill turned and started jogging back, saw Chris and Barry do the same. Wesker was still by the helicopter and had drawn his weapon at Joseph's cry, pointing it up as he broke into a run.

In the murky light, Jill could just make out Joseph's shadowy form, crouched down in the high grass near some trees a hundred feet past the 'copter. Instinctively, she pulled her own sidearm and double-timed, suddenly overwhelmed by a sense of encroaching doom.

Joseph stood up, holding something, and let out a strangled scream before dropping it, his eyes wide with horror.

For a split-second, Jill's mind couldn't accept what it had seen in Joseph's grasp.

A S.T.A.R.S. handgun, a Beretta—

Jill ran faster, catching up to Wesker.

—and a disembodied human hand curled around it, hacked off at the wrist.

There was a deep, guttural snarl from behind Joseph, from the darkness of the trees. An animal, growling—

—joined by another rasping, throaty shriek—

49

—and suddenly dark, powerful shapes erupted from the woods, lunging at Joseph and taking him down.

"Joseph!"

Jill's scream ringing in his ears, Chris drew his weapon and stopped in his tracks, trying to get a clear shot at the raging beasts that were attacking Joseph. Wesker's penlight sent a thin beam dancing over the writhing creatures, illuminating a nightmare.

Joseph's body was all but hidden by the three animals that tore at him, ripping at him with gnashing, dripping jaws. They were the size and shape of dogs, as big as German shepherds maybe, except that they seemed to have no fur, no *skin*. Wet, red sinew and muscle flashed beneath Wesker's wavering light, the dog-creatures shrieking and snapping in a frenzy of bloodlust.

Joseph cried out, a burbling, liquid sound as he flailed weakly at the savage attackers, blood pouring from multiple wounds. It was the scream of a dying man. There was no time to waste; Chris targeted and opened fire.

Three rounds smacked wetly into one of the dogs, a fourth shot going high. There was a single, high-pitched yelp and the beast went down, its sides heaving. The other two animals continued their assault, indifferent to the thunderous shots. Even as Chris watched in horror, one of the slavering hell hounds lunged forward and ripped out Joseph's throat, exposing bloody gristle and the glistening slickness of bone.

The S.T.A.R.S. opened up, sending a rain of explosive fire at Joseph's killers. Red spatters burst into the air, the dog-things still trying to get at the spasming corpse while bullets riddled their strange flesh. With a final series of harsh, barking mewls, they fell—and didn't rise again.

"Hold your fire!"

Chris took his finger off the trigger but continued to point the handgun at the fallen creatures, ready to blow apart the first one that so much as twitched. Two of them were still breathing, growling softly through panting gasps. The third sprawled lifelessly next to Joseph's mutilated body.

—*they should be dead, should've stayed down at the first shots! What are they?*

Wesker took a single step toward the slaughter in front of them—

—when all around, deep, echoing howls filled the warm night air, shrill voices of predatorial fury coming at the S.T.A.R.S. from all directions.

"Back to the 'copter, *now!*" Wesker shouted.

Chris ran, Barry and Jill in front of him and Wesker bringing up the rear. The four of them sprinted through dark trees, unseen branches slapping at them as the howls grew louder, more insistent.

Wesker turned and fired blindly into the woods as they stumbled toward the waiting helicopter, its blades already spinning. Chris felt relief sweep through him; Brad must have heard the shots. They still had a chance. . . .

Chris could hear the creatures behind them now, the sharp rustling of lean, muscular bodies tearing through the trees. He could also see Brad's pale, wide-eyed face through the glass front of the 'copter, the reflected lights of the control panel casting a greenish glow across his panicked features. He was shouting something, but the roar of the engine drowned out everything now, the blast of wind churning the field into a rippling sea.

Another fifty feet, almost there—

Suddenly, the helicopter jerked into the air, accelerating wildly. Chris caught a final glimpse of Brad's face and could see the blind terror there, the unthinking panic that had gripped him as he clawed at the controls.

"No! Don't go!" Chris screamed, but the wobbling rails were already out of reach, the 'copter pitching forward and away from them through the thundering darkness.

They were going to die.

Damn you, Vickers!

Wesker turned and fired again, and was rewarded with a squeal of pain from one of their pursuers. There were at least four more close behind, gaining on them rapidly.

"Keep going!" he shouted, trying to get his bearings as they stumbled on, the piercing shrieks of the mutant dogs urging them faster. The sound of the helicopter was dying away, the cowardly Vickers taking their escape with him.

Wesker fired again, the shot going wide, and saw another shadowy form join the hunt. The dogs were brutally fast. They didn't stand a chance, unless . . .

The mansion!

"Veer right, one o'clock!" Wesker yelled, hoping that his sense of direction was still intact. They couldn't outrun the creatures, but maybe they could keep them at bay long enough to reach cover.

He spun and fired the last round in his clip. "Empty!"

Ejecting the spent magazine, he fumbled for another one tucked into his belt as both Barry and Chris took up the defense, firing past him and into the closing pack. Wesker slapped in the fresh clip as they reached the edge of the overgrown clearing and plunged into another dark stand of trees.

They stumbled and dodged through the woods, tripping on uneven ground as the killer dogs came on. Lungs aching for air, Wesker imagined that he could smell the fetid, rotting-meat stench of the beasts as they narrowed the distance and he somehow found the capacity to run faster.

We should be there by now, gotta be close—

Chris saw it first through the thinning shadows of trees, the looming monstrosity back-lit by an early moon. "There! Run for that house!"

It looked abandoned from the outside, the weathered wood and stone of the giant mansion crumbling and dark. The full size of the structure was cloaked by the shadowy, overgrown hedges that surrounded it, isolating it from the forest. A massive outset front porch presented double doors, their only option for escape.

Wesker actually heard the snap of powerful jaws behind him and fired at the sound, intuitively squeezing the trigger as he ran for the front of the mansion.

A gurgling yelp and the creature fell away, the howls of its siblings louder than ever, raised to a fever pitch by the thrill of the chase.

Jill reached the doors first, slamming into the heavy wood with one shoulder as she snatched at the handles. Amazingly, they crashed open; brightness spilled out across the stone steps to the porch, lighting their path. She turned and started firing, providing cover as the three gasping men ran for the opening in the darkness.

They piled into the mansion, Jill diving in last and Barry throwing his considerable bulk against the door, wedging it closed against the snarls of the creatures. He collapsed against it, face red and sweating, as Chris found the entry's steel deadbolt and slid it home.

They'd made it. Outside, the dogs howled and scrabbled uselessly at the heavy doors.

Wesker took a deep breath of the cool, quiet air that filled the well-lit room and exhaled sharply. As he'd already known, the Spencer house wasn't abandoned. And now that they were here, all his careful planning was for nothing.

Wesker silently cursed Brad Vickers again and wondered if they were any better off inside than out. . . .

FIVE

JILL TOOK IN THEIR NEW SURROUNDINGS AS
she caught her breath, feeling like she was a character
in a nightmare that had just taken a turn into grand
fantasy. Wild, howling monsters, Joseph's sudden
death, a terrifying run through the dark woods—and
now this.

Deserted, huh?

It was a palace, pure and simple, what her father
would have called a perfect score. The room they had
escaped into was the epitome of lavish. It was huge,
easily bigger than Jill's entire house, tiled in gray-
flecked marble and dominated by a wide, carpeted
staircase that led to a second-floor balcony. Arched
marble pillars lined the ornate hall, supporting the
dark, heavy wood balustrade of the upper floor.
Fluted wall sconces cast funnels of light across walls

of cream, trimmed in oak and offset by the deep burnt ocher of the carpeting. In short, it was magnificent.

"What *is* this?" Barry muttered. No one answered him.

Jill took a deep breath and decided immediately that she didn't like it. There was a sense of . . . *wrongness* to the vast room, an atmosphere of vague oppression. It felt haunted somehow, though by who or what, she couldn't say.

Beats the hell out of getting eaten by mutant dogs, though, gotta give it that much. And on the trail of that thought, *God, poor Joseph!* There hadn't been time to mourn him, and there wasn't time now—but he would be missed.

She walked toward the stairs clutching her handgun, her footsteps muffled by the plush carpet that led from the front door. There was an antique typewriter on a small table to the right of the steps, a blank sheet of paper spooled into the works. A strange bit of a decorum. The expansive hall was otherwise empty.

She turned back toward the others, wondering what their take on all this was. Barry and Chris both looked uncertain, their faces flushed and sweaty as they surveyed the room. Wesker was crouched by the front door, examining one of the latches.

He stood up, his dark shades still in place, seeming as detached as ever. "The wood around the lock is splintered. Somebody broke this door open before we got here."

Chris looked hopeful. "Maybe the Bravos?"

Wesker nodded. "That's what I'm thinking. Help

should be on the way, assuming our 'friend' Mr. Vickers bothers to call it in."

His voice dripped sarcasm, and Jill felt her own anger kindling. Brad had screwed up big time, had almost cost them their lives. There was no excuse for what he'd done.

Wesker continued, walking across the room toward one of the two doors on the west wall. He rattled the handle, but it didn't open. "It's not safe to go back out. Until the cavalry shows up, we might as well take a look around. It's obvious that somebody's been keeping this place up, though why and for how long . . ."

He trailed off, walking back toward the group. "How are we set for ammo?"

Jill ejected the clip from her Beretta and counted: three rounds left, plus the two loaded magazines on her belt. Thirty-three shots. Chris had twenty-two left, Wesker, seventeen. Barry had two racked speed loaders for his Colt, plus an extra handful of loose cartridges tucked into a hip pouch, nineteen rounds in all.

Jill thought about all they'd left back on the helicopter and felt another rush of anger toward Brad. Boxes of ammunition, flashlights, walkie-talkies, shotguns—not to mention medical supplies. That Beretta that Joseph had found out in the field, the pale, blood-spattered fingers still wrapped around it—a S.T.A.R.S. team member dead or dying, and thanks to Brad, they didn't even have a band-aid to offer.

Thump!

A sound of something heavy sliding to the floor, somewhere close by. In unison, they turned toward the single door on the east wall. Jill was suddenly reminded of every horror movie she'd ever seen; a strange house, a strange noise . . . she shivered, and decided that she was most definitely going to kick Brad's narrow ass when they got out of here.

"Chris, check it out and report back ASAP," Wesker said. "We'll wait here in case the RPD comes knocking. You run into any trouble, fire your weapon and we'll find you."

Chris nodded and started toward the door, his boots clacking loudly against the marble floor.

Jill felt that sense of foreboding wash over her again. "Chris?"

His hand on the knob, he turned back, and she realized that there was nothing she could tell him that made any sense. Everything was happening so fast, there was so much wrong with this situation that she didn't know where to start—

And he's a trained professional, and so are you. Start acting like it.

"Take care," she said finally. It wasn't what she wanted to say, but it'd have to be enough.

Chris gave her a lopsided grin, then raised his Beretta and stepped through the doorway. Jill heard the ticking of a clock and then he was gone, closing the door behind him.

Barry caught her gaze and smiled at her, a look that told her not to worry—but Jill couldn't shake the sudden certainty that Chris wouldn't be coming back.

* * *

Chris swept the room, taking in the stately elegance of the environment as he realized he was alone; whoever had made the noise, they weren't here.

The solemn ticking of a grandfather clock filled the cool air, echoing off of shining black and white tiles. He was in a dining hall, the kind he'd only ever seen in movies about rich people. Like the front room, this one had an incredibly high ceiling and a second-floor balcony, but it was also decorated with expensive-looking art and had an inset fireplace at the far end, complete with a coat of arms and crossed swords hung over the mantle. There didn't seem to be any way to get to the second floor, but there was a closed door to the right of the fireplace. . . .

Chris lowered his weapon and started for the door, still awed by the wealth of the "abandoned" mansion that the S.T.A.R.S. had stumbled into. The dining room had polished red wood trim and expensive looking artwork on the beige stucco walls, surrounding a long wooden table that ran the length of the room. The table had to seat at least twenty, though it was only set for a handful of people. Judging from the dust on the lacy place mats, nothing had been served for weeks.

Except no one is supposed to have been here for thirty years, let alone hosted a formal dinner! Spencer had this place closed down before anyone ever stayed here—

Chris shook his head. Obviously someone had reopened it a long time ago . . . so how was it that everyone in Raccoon City believed the Spencer estate to be boarded up, a crumbling ruin out in the woods?

More importantly, why had Umbrella lied to Irons about its condition?

Murders, disappearances, Umbrella, Jill. . . . It was frustrating; he felt like he had some of the answers, but wasn't sure what questions to ask.

He reached the door and turned the knob slowly, listening for any sound of movement on the other side. He couldn't hear anything over the ticking of the old clock; it was set against the wall and each movement of the second hand reverberated hollowly, amplified by the cavernous room.

The door opened into one side of a narrow corridor, dimly lit by antique light fixtures. Chris quickly checked both directions. To the right was maybe ten meters of hardwood hall, a couple of doors across from him and a door at the end of the corridor. To the left, the hallway took a sharp turn away from where he stood, widening out. He saw the edge of a patterned brown run on the floor there.

He wrinkled his nose, frowning. There was a vague odor in the air, a faint scent of something unpleasant—something *familiar*. He stood in the doorway another moment, trying to place the smell.

One summer when he was a kid, the chain had come off his bike when he'd been out on a ride with some friends. He'd ended up in a ditch about six inches away from a choice bit of roadkill, the dried-up, pulpy remains of what once might have been a woodchuck. Time and the summer heat had dissipated the worst of the stink, though what had remained had been bad enough. Much to the amusement of his buddies, he'd vomited his lunch all over the carcass, taken a deep breath, then puked again. He still remembered the sun-baked scent of drying rot, like thickly soured milk and bile; the same smell that lingered in the corridor now like a bad dream.

Fummp.

A soft, shuffling noise from behind the first door to his right, like a padded fist sliding across a wall. There was someone on the other side.

Chris edged into the hallway and moved toward the door, careful not to turn his back to the unsecured area. As he got closer, the gentle sounds of movement stopped, and he could see that the door wasn't closed all the way.

No time like the present.

With an easy tap the door swung inward, into a dim hall with green flecked wallpaper. A broad-shouldered man was standing not twenty feet away, half-hidden in shadow, his back to Chris. He turned around slowly, the careful shuffling of someone drunk or injured, and the smell that Chris had noticed before came off of the man in thick, noxious waves. His clothes were tattered and stained, the back of his head patchy with sparse, scraggly hair.

Gotta be sick, dying maybe—

Whatever was wrong with him, Chris didn't like it; his instincts were screaming at him to do something. He stepped into the corridor and trained his Beretta on the man's torso. "Hold it, don't move!"

The man completed his turn and started toward Chris, shambling forward into the light. His—*its*—face was deathly pale, except for the blood smeared around its rotting lips. Flaps of dried skin hung from its sunken cheeks, and the dark wells of the creature's eye sockets glittered with hunger as it reached out with skeletal hands—

Chris fired, three shots that smacked into the creature's upper chest in a fine spray of crimson. With a gasping moan, it crumpled to the floor, dead.

Chris staggered back, his thoughts racing in time with his hammering heart. He hit the door with one shoulder, was vaguely aware that it latched closed behind him as he stared at the fallen, stinking heap.

—dead, that thing's the walking-goddamn-dead!

The cannibal attacks in Raccoon, all of them near the forest. He'd seen enough late-night movies to know what he was looking at, but he still couldn't believe it.

Zombies.

No, no way, that was fiction—but maybe some kind of a disease, mimicking the symptoms. He had to tell the others. He turned and grabbed at the handle, but the heavy door wouldn't move, it must have locked itself when he'd stumbled—

Behind him, a wet movement. Chris spun, eyes wide as the twitching creature clawed at the wooden floor, pulling itself toward him in an eager, single-minded silence. Chris realized that it was drooling, and the sight of the sticky pink rivulets pooling to the wood floor finally spurred him to action.

He fired again, two shots into the thing's decaying, upturned face. Dark holes opened up in its knobby skull, sending tiny rivers of fluid and fleshy tissue through its lower jaw. With a heavy sigh, the rotting thing settled to the floor in a spreading red lake.

Chris didn't want to make any bets on it staying down. He gave one more futile yank on the door and then stepped carefully past the body, moving down the corridor. He rattled the handle of a door on his left, but it was locked. There was a tiny etching in the key plate, what looked like a sword; he filed that bit of information into his confused, whirling thoughts and continued on, gripping the Beretta tightly.

There was an offshoot to his right with a single door, but he ignored it, wanting to find a way to circle back to the front hall. The others must have heard the shots, but he had to assume that there were more creatures running around here like the one he'd killed. The rest of the team might already have their hands full.

There was a door at the end of the hall on the left, where the corridor turned. Chris hurried toward it, the putrid scent of the creature—

—*the zombie, call it what it is*—

—making him want to gag. As he neared the door, he realized that the smell was actually getting worse, intensifying with each step.

He heard the soft, hungry moan as his hand touched the knob, even as it registered that he only had two bullets left in his clip. In the shadows to his right, movement.

Gotta reload, get somewhere safe—

Chris jerked the door open and stepped into the arms of the shambling creature that waited on the other side, its peeling fingers grasping at him as it lunged for his throat.

Three shots. Seconds later, two more, the sounds distant but distinct in the palatial lobby.

Chris!

"Jill, why don't you—" Wesker started, but Barry didn't let him finish.

"I'm going, too," he said, already starting for the door on the east wall. Chris wouldn't waste shots like that unless he had to; he needed help.

Wesker relented quickly, nodding. "Go. I'll wait here."

Barry opened the door, Jill right behind. They walked into a huge dining room, not as wide as the front hall but at least as long. There was another door at the opposite end, past a grandfather clock that ticked loudly in the frigid, dusty air.

Barry jogged toward it, revolver in hand, feeling tense and worried. Christ, what a balls-up this operation was! S.T.A.R.S. teams were often sent into risky situations where the circumstances were unusual, but this was the first time since he'd been a rookie that Barry felt like things had gone totally out of control. Joseph was dead, Chickenheart Vickers had left them to be eaten by dogs from hell, and now Chris was in trouble. Wesker shouldn't have sent him in alone.

Jill reached the door first, touching the handle with slim fingers and looking to him. Barry nodded and she pushed it open, going in low and left.

Barry took the other side, both of them sweeping an empty corridor.

"Chris?" Jill called out quietly, but there was no answer. Barry scowled, sniffing the air; something smelled like rotting fruit.

"I'll check the doors," Barry said. Jill nodded and edged to the left, alert and focused.

Barry moved toward the first door, feeling good that Jill was at his back. He'd thought she was kind of bitchy when she'd first transferred, but she was proving to be a bright and capable soldier, a welcome addition to the Alphas—

Jill let out a high-pitched gasp of surprise and Barry spun, the scent of decay suddenly thick in the narrow hall.

Jill was backing away from an opening at the end of the corridor, her weapon trained on something Barry couldn't see.

"Stop!" Her voice was high and shaky, her expression horrified—

—and she fired, once, twice, still backing toward Barry, her breathing fast and shallow.

"Get clear, left!" He raised the Colt as she moved out of the way, as a tall man stepped into view. The figure's arms were stretched out like a sleepwalker's, the hands frail and grasping.

Barry saw the creature's face then and didn't hesitate. He fired, a .357 round peeling the top of its ashen skull away in an explosive burst, blood coursing down its strange, terrible features and staining the cataracts of its pale, rolling eyes.

It pitched back, sprawling face-up at Jill's feet. Barry hurried to her side, stunned.

"What—" he started, then saw what was on the

carpet in front of them, laying in the small sitting area that marked the end of the corridor.

For a moment, Barry thought it was Chris—until he saw the S.T.A.R.S. Bravo insignia on the vest, and felt a different kind of horror set in as he struggled to recognize the features. The Bravo had been decapitated, the head laying a foot away from the corpse, the face completely covered in gore.

Oh jeez, it's Ken.

Kenneth Sullivan, one of the best field scouts Barry had ever known and a hell of a nice guy. There was a gaping, ragged wound in his chest, chunks of partly eaten tissue and gut strewn around the bloody hole. His left hand was missing, and there was no weapon nearby; it must have been his gun that Joseph had found out in the woods. . . .

Barry looked away, sickened. Ken had been a quiet, decent sort, did a lot of work in chemistry. He'd had a teen-aged son who lived with his ex in California. Barry thought of his own girls at home, Moira and Poly, and felt a surge of helpless fear for them. He wasn't afraid of death, but the thought of them growing up without a father. . . .

Jill dropped into a crouch next to his ravaged body and rifled quickly through the belt pack. She shot an apologetic look at Barry, but he gave her a slight nod. They needed the ammo; Ken certainly didn't.

She came up with two clips for a nine-millimeter and tucked them into her hip pocket. Barry turned and stared down at Ken's murderer in disgust and wonder.

He had no doubt that he was looking at one of the

cannibal killers that had been preying upon Raccoon City. It had a crusty scum of red around its mouth and gore-encrusted nails, as well as a ragged shirt that was stiff with dried blood. What was weird was how— *dead* it looked.

Barry had once done a covert hostage rescue in Ecuador, where a group of farmers had been held for weeks by a band of insane guerrilla rebels. Several of the hostages had been killed early in the siege, and after the S.T.A.R.S. managed to capture the rebels, Barry had gone with one of the survivors to record the deaths. The four victims had been shot, their bodies dumped behind the small wooden shack that the rebels had taken over. After three weeks in the South American sun, the skin on their faces had shriveled, the cracking, lined flesh pulling away from sinew and bone. He still remembered those faces clearly, and saw them again now as he looked down at the fallen creature. It wore the face of death.

Besides which, it smells like a slaughterhouse on a hot day. Somebody forgot to tell this guy that dead people don't walk around.

He could see the same sickened confusion on Jill's face, the same questions in her eyes, but for now, there weren't any answers; they had to find Chris and regroup.

Together, they moved back down the corridor and checked all three doors, rattling handles and pushing at the heavy wood frames. All were securely locked.

But Chris had to have gone through one of them, there's nowhere else he could have gone. . . .

It didn't make sense, and short of breaking the doors down, there was nothing they could do about it.

"We should report this to Wesker," Jill said, and Barry nodded agreement. If they'd stumbled into the hiding place of the killers, they were going to need a plan of attack.

They ran back through the dining room, the stale air a relief after the corridor's reek of blood and decay. They reached the door back to the main hall and hurried through, Barry wondering what the captain would make of all this. It was downright—

Barry stopped short, searching the elegant, empty hall and feeling like the butt of some practical joke that simply wasn't funny.

Wesker was gone.

Six

"WESKER!" BARRY SHOUTED, HIS DEEP VOICE echoing through the chilly room. "Captain Wesker!"

He jogged toward a row of arches at the back of the hall, calling to Jill over his shoulder as he ran. "Don't leave the room!"

Jill walked to the stairs, feeling almost dizzy. First Chris, now the captain. They hadn't been gone five minutes and he'd said he was going to stay put. Why would he have left? She looked around for signs of a struggle, a spent cartridge, a spot of blood—there was nothing to indicate what might have happened.

Barry appeared on the other side of the giant staircase, shaking his head and walking slowly to join her. Jill bit her lower lip, frowning.

"You think Wesker ran into one of those—things?" she asked.

Barry sighed. "I don't think the RPD showed and snuck him out. Though if he *did* run into trouble, we would have heard the shots—"

"Not necessarily. He could have been ambushed, dragged away . . ."

They stood silently for a moment, thinking. Jill was still a bit shaken from the face-to-face with the walking corpse, but thought she'd accepted the facts pretty well; the woods bordering Raccoon City had become infested with zombies.

After a lifetime of reading trashy novels about serial killers, is a cannibal zombie so hard to swallow? Somehow it wasn't, and neither were the murderous dogs or the secretly kept estate. There was no question that it all existed. The question was, why? Did the mansion have anything to do with the murders, or had the zombies simply overrun it like they'd overrun Raccoon Forest?

And was that creature the last thing Becky and Pris saw?

She rejected that thought almost violently; thinking about the girls now would be a mistake.

"So do we go looking or do we wait?" Jill said finally.

"Go looking. Ken made it here. The rest of the Bravos could be somewhere in this house. It'd be easy enough to get lost. Chris . . ."

He half-smiled, though Jill could see the worry in his eyes. "Chris and Wesker got—side-tracked, but we'll find them. It'd take more than a couple of walking stiffs to cause either of them any grief."

He reached into a pocket in his vest and pulled out

something wrapped in a handkerchief, handing it to her. She felt the thin metal objects beneath the light fabric and recognized them instantly.

"It's the set you gave me to practice with last month," he said. "I figure you'll have better luck with them."

Jill nodded, tucking the lockpicks into her hip pouch. Barry had taken an interest in her former "career" and she'd given him a few pieces from her old set, several picks and torsion bars. They could come in handy. The small bundle settled on top of something hard and smooth—

—*Trent's computer!* In all the excitement, she'd totally forgotten about her strange encounter in the locker room. She opened her mouth to tell Barry, then shut it, remembering Trent's cryptic warning.

"I wouldn't mention this conversation to anyone."

Screw that. She'd almost risked it anyway with Chris. . . .

And where is Chris now? Who's to say that Trent's "dire consequences" haven't already occurred?

Jill realized what she was thinking and had to fight off an urge to laugh at herself. What had happened with Trent probably wasn't even relevant to their predicament, and whether or not she could trust Barry, she *knew* she didn't trust Trent—still, she decided not to say anything about it, at least until she had a chance to see what the computer held.

"I think we should split up," Barry continued. "I know it's dangerous, but we need to cover a lot of ground. We find anybody, we meet back here, use this room as base."

Rubbing at his beard, he fixed her with a serious gaze. "You up for this, Jill? We could search together . . ."

"No, you're right," she said. "I can take the west wing." Unlike cops, S.T.A.R.S. seldom partnered. They were trained to watch their own backs in dangerous situations.

Barry nodded. "Okay. I'll go back and see if I can persuade one of those doors to open. Keep an eye out for a back exit, conserve ammo . . and be careful."

"You, too."

Barry grinned, holding up his Colt Python. "I'll be fine."

There was nothing left to say. Jill headed straight for the set of doors on the west wall that Wesker hadn't tried earlier. Behind her, Barry hurried back to the dining room. She heard the door open and close, leaving her alone.

Here goes nothing.

The painted blue doors opened smoothly, revealing a small, shadowy room as cool and silent as the main hall, all in shades of blue. Muted track lighting illuminated framed paintings on dusky walls, and in the center of the room was a large statue of a woman holding an urn on one shoulder.

Jill closed the door behind her and let her eyes adjust to the gloom, noting the two doors opposite the one she'd come through. The one on the left was open, though a small chest was pushed in front of it, blocking access. It was unlikely that Wesker had gone that way. . . .

She walked to the one on the right and tried the

knob. Locked. Sighing, she reached into her pack for the picks and then hesitated, feeling the smooth weight of the mini-disk reader.

Let's see what Mr. Trent thinks is so important....

She slipped it out and studied it a moment, then tapped at a switch. A screen the size of a baseball card flickered to life, and with a few more taps, small lines of type scrolled across the monitor. She scanned the material, recognizing names and dates from local newspapers. Trent had apparently compiled every article he could find about the murders and disappearances in Raccoon, plus the pieces on the S.T.A.R.S.

Nothing new here.... Jill skipped along, wondering what the point was. After the articles was a list of names.

WILLIAM BIRKIN, STEVE KELLER, MICHAEL DEES, JOHN HOWE, MARTIN CRACKHORN, HENRY SARTON, ELLEN SMITH, BILL RABBITSON

She frowned. None of the names were familiar, except—wasn't Bill Rabbitson Chris's friend, the one who had worked for Umbrella? She couldn't be sure, she'd have to ask Chris....

... assuming we find him. This was a waste of time; she needed to start looking for the other S.T.A.R.S. She pressed the forwarding key to get to the end of the data and a picture appeared, tiny lines set into patterns. There were squares and long rectangles, crosshatched with smaller marks that connected the empty boxes. Beneath it was a single line, a message as enigmatic as she could have expected from Mr. Trent:

KNIGHT KEYS; TIGER EYES; FOUR CRESTS (GATE OF NEW LIFE); EAST-EAGLE/WEST-WOLF.

Gee, how illuminating. That just clears up everything, doesn't it? The picture was some kind of map, she decided. It looked like a floor plan. The biggest area was at the center, a slightly smaller one extending off to the left. . . .

Jill suddenly felt her heart skip a beat. She stared down at the small screen, wondering how Trent had known.

It was the mansion's first floor. She tapped the forward button again and saw what could only be the second floor, the shapes corresponding to the first map. There was nothing after the second map, but it was enough.

As far as she was concerned, there was no longer any question that the Spencer estate was the source of the terror in Raccoon City—which meant that the answers were here, waiting to be uncovered.

The zombie groaned as Chris fired point-blank into its gut, twice. The shots were muffled by its rancid flesh and it fell against him, expelling a rush of foul, stinking air across his face.

Chris pushed it away, the back of his throat locking. His hands and the barrel of his weapon were dripping with sticky fluids. The creature collapsed to the floor, its limbs spasming.

Chris backed away, wiping the Beretta against his vest as he took deep breaths, trying desperately not to vomit. The zombie out in the hall had been a desiccated mess, shriveled and dry; this one was—fresh, if that was the right word. Festering, necrotic, wet . . .

He swallowed, hard, and the urge to throw up slowly passed. He didn't have a particularly weak stomach, but that *smell*, God!

Keep it together, could be more of them. . . .

The hall he'd entered was all dark wood and dim light. For the moment, there was no sound except the pulse of blood in his ears. He looked down at the body, wondering exactly what it was, what it had been. He had felt its hot, fetid breath against his face. It wasn't a reanimated corpse, no matter what it looked like.

He decided it didn't matter. For all intents and purposes, it was a zombie. It had tried to bite him, and creatures like it had already chowed down on some of Raccoon's population. He needed to find his way back to the others and they had to get out, get help. They didn't have the firepower to handle the situation alone.

He ejected the empty clip from the gummy weapon and quickly reloaded, his chest tightening with stress; fifteen rounds left. He had a Bowie knife, but the thought of going up against a zombie with only a knife wasn't all that appealing.

There was a plain-looking door to his left. Chris pulled at the knob, but it was locked. He squinted at the key plate, and wasn't all that surprised to see an etching of what looked like armor. Sword, armor— there was a definite theme developing.

He moved down the wide hall, listening for any sound and taking frequent deep breaths through his nose. The goo on his vest and hands made it hard to tell if there were any more of them around, the smell was all over him, but it could be his only chance to avoid another close encounter.

The hall turned to the left and he took the corner fast, sweeping the Beretta across the wide wooden expanse. There was a support pillar partially blocking his view but he could see the back of a man just past it, the slumped shoulders and stained clothes of one of the creatures.

Chris quickly edged to the right, trying to get a clear shot. The zombie was maybe forty feet away, and he didn't want to waste his last rounds. At the sound of his boots against the hard wood floor, it turned, shuffling slowly. So slowly that Chris hesitated, watching the way it moved.

This one seemed to have been dipped in a thin layer of slime, dull light reflecting off of its glistening skin as it stumbled almost blindly toward Chris. It slowly raised its arms, its pale, hairless skull wobbling on its emaciated neck. Silently, it shuffled forward.

Chris took a sliding step back to his left and the zombie changed direction, veering toward him eagerly, closing the distance between them at a slow walk.

Just like in the movies; dangerous but dumb. And easy to outrun. . . .

He had to save ammo in case he got cornered. There were stairs at the end of the hall, and Chris took a deep breath, readying himself. He stepped back, giving himself enough room to maneuver—

—and heard a gasping moan behind him, a fresh wave of rancid stink assaulting his senses. He spun, the realization hitting him even before he saw it.

The festering zombie was only a few feet away, reaching for him, bits of its putrid gut spilling out across its shattered abdomen. He hadn't killed it, hadn't waited long enough to make sure, and his stupidity was about to cost him.

Ah, shit!

Chris sprinted away and down the corridor, dodging both of them and cursing himself. He passed the thick support beam, almost to the stairs—

—and stopped cold, seeing what waited at the top. He caught only a glimpse of the ragged creature standing at the head of the stairs and spun away, raising his weapon to face the attackers that shambled toward him hungrily.

From the shadows beneath the steps came a heavy, gurgling sigh and the scuffing of wood; another one. He was trapped, there was no way he could kill them all—

—*door!*

It faced the side of the stairs, the dark wood blending so well with the shadows that he almost hadn't seen it. Chris ran for it, grabbing at the handle, praying that it would open as around him, the creatures closed in.

If it was locked, he was dead.

Rebecca Chambers had never been more afraid, not once in her eighteen years. For what seemed like an eternity, she'd listened to the soft scrape of rotting flesh brushing against the door and tried desperately to think of a plan, her dread building with each passing minute. There was no lock on the door, and she'd lost her handgun on the run for the house. The small storage room, though well stocked with chemicals and stacks of papers, had offered nothing to use as a defense except a half-empty can of insect repellent.

It was the can she gripped now, standing behind the door of the tiny room. If or when the monsters finally figured out how to use a doorknob, she planned on spraying it in their eyes and then making a run for it.

Maybe they'll be laughing so hard I'll have a chance to slip past; bug spray, great weapon. . . .

She'd heard what could have been shots somewhere close by, but they weren't repeated. Her hope that it was one of the team faded as the seconds ticked past, and she was starting to give serious consideration to the concept that she was the only one left when the door burst open and a gasping figure hurdled inside.

Rebecca didn't hesitate. She leapt forward and pressed the button, releasing a cloud of chemical mist into its face, tensing herself to run past it—

"Gah!" It yelled, and fell back against the door, slamming it shut. It covered its eyes, spluttering.

It wasn't a monster; she'd just maced one of the Alphas.

"Oh, no!" Rebecca was already reaching into her field medical kit, her immense relief at seeing another of the S.T.A.R.S. battling with monumental embarrassment.

She fumbled out a clean cloth and a tiny squeeze bottle of water, stepping toward him. "Keep your eyes closed, don't rub at them."

The Alpha dropped his hands, face red, and she finally recognized him. It was Chris Redfield, only the most attractive guy in the S.T.A.R.S., not to mention her superior. She felt herself blush, and was suddenly glad that he couldn't see her.

Nice going, Rebecca. Way to make a good impression on your first operation. Lose your gun, get lost, blind a teammate . . .

She led him over to the small cot in the corner of the room and sat him down, letting her training take over.

"Lean your head back. This is going to sting a little, but it's just water, okay?" She dabbed at his eyes with the damp cloth, relieved that she hadn't sprayed him with anything worse.

"What was that stuff?" he said, blinking rapidly. Tears and water streamed down his face, but there didn't seem to be any damage.

"Uh, bug repellent. The label's been ripped off but the active ingredient is probably permephrin, it's an irritant but the effect shouldn't last long. I lost my gun, and when you came in I thought you were one of those things, though if they haven't figured out how to use a doorknob by now, they probably won't—"

She realized she was babbling and shut up, finishing the crude irrigation and stepping back. Chris wiped at his face and peered up at her with bloodshot eyes.

"Rebecca . . . Chambers, right?"

She nodded miserably. "Yeah. Look, I'm really sorry—"

"Don't worry about it," he said, and smiled. "Not a bad weapon, actually."

He stood up and looked around the small room, frowning. There wasn't much to see: an open trunk full of papers, a shelf lined with bottles of mostly unlabeled chemicals, a cot, and a desk. Rebecca had been through it all in her search for something to use against the creatures.

"What about the rest of your team?" he asked.

Rebecca shook her head. "I don't know. Something went wrong with the helicopter and we had to set down. We were attacked by animals, some kind of dogs, and Enrico told us to run for cover."

She shrugged, suddenly feeling like she was about twelve years old. "I got—turned around in the woods and ended up at the front door of this place. I think one of the others broke it down, it was open . . ."

She trailed off, looking away from his intense gaze. The rest was probably obvious: she had no weapon, she'd gotten lost, she'd ended up here. All in all, a pretty poor showing.

"Hey," he said softly. "There's nothing else you could have done. Enrico said run, you ran, you followed orders. Those creatures out there, the zombies . . . they're all over the place. I got lost, too, and the rest of the Alphas could be anywhere. Trust me, just the fact that you made it this far—"

Outside, one of the monsters let out a low, plaintive wail and Chris stopped talking, his expression grim.

Rebecca shuddered. "So what do we do now?"

"We look for the others and try to find a way out." He sighed, looking down at his weapon. "Except you don't have a gun and I'm almost out of ammo. . . ."

Rebecca brightened and reached into her hip pack. She pulled out two full magazines and handed them over, pleased that she had something to offer him.

"Oh! And I found this on the desk," she said, and produced a silver key with a sword on it. She didn't know what it unlocked, but thought it might be useful. Chris stared at it thoughtfully, then slipped it into a pocket. He walked to the open trunk and looked down at the stacks of papers. He rifled through them, frowning.

"Your background's in biochemistry, right? Have you looked through these?"

Rebecca joined him, shaking her head. "Barely. I've been kinda busy watching the door."

He handed her one of the papers and she scanned it quickly. It was a list of neurotransmitters and level indicators.

"Brain chemistry," she said, "but these numbers are all screwed up. The serotonin and norepinephrine are too low . . . but look here, the dopamine is off the chart, we're talking big-time schizo—"

She noticed the incredulous look on his face and smiled a little. Being an eighteen-year-old college grad, she got a lot of that. The S.T.A.R.S. had recruited her right after graduation, promising her a whole team of researchers and a lab of her own to study molecular biology, her real passion—provided, of course, that she went through basic training and got some field experience. No one else had shown much interest in hiring a whiz kid. . . .

There was a soft *thump* at the door and her smile faded. She was getting experience, alright.

Chris fished the sword key out of his pocket and looked at her seriously. "I passed a door with a sword engraved over the keyhole. I'm going to go check it out, see if it leads back to the main hall. I want you to stay here and go through those files. Maybe there's something we can use."

Her uncertainty must have showed in her face. He smiled gently, his voice low and soothing. "I've got plenty of ammo, thanks to you, and I won't be gone long."

She nodded, making a conscious effort to relax. She was scared, but letting him see it wasn't going to help matters. He was probably scared, too.

He walked to the door, still talking. "The RPD should be here any time, so if I don't come back right away, just wait here."

He raised the weapon, putting his other hand on the knob. "Get ready. As soon as I'm out, move the trunk in front of the door. I'll give a yell when I get back."

Rebecca nodded again, and with a final quick smile, Chris opened the door and looked both ways before moving out into the hall. She closed the door and leaned against it, listening. After long seconds of silence, she heard the rattle of gunfire not far away, five or six shots—then nothing.

After a few minutes, she moved the trunk to block part of the door, edging it in front of the hinges so she could push it out of the way easily. She knelt in front of it, trying to clear her thoughts as she started looking through the papers, trying not to feel as young and unsure as she actually felt.

Sighing, she pulled out a handful of papers and started to read.

SEVEⅡ

THE LOCK WAS A PIECE OF CAKE, THREE FLAT
tumblers in a single row; Jill could have opened it with
a couple of paper clips. According to the map, the door
would open into a long hall. . . .

Sure enough. She took another long look at the
pocket computer's screen and then slipped it into her
pack, thinking. It looked like there was a back way
out, through several halls and past a series of rooms.
She could look for Wesker and the others along the
way, and maybe secure an escape route at the same
time. She stepped into the narrow corridor, the fully
loaded Beretta in hand.

It was a study in weirdness. The hall wasn't all that
spectacular, the carpet runner and the wallpaper done
in basic tans and browns, the wide windows showing

only the darkness outside. The display chests that lined the inner wall, though . . .

There were three of them, each topped by a small lamp, and each prominently displaying a wide array of bleached human bones on open shelves, interspersed with small items of obscurity. Jill started down the hall, stopping briefly at each bizarre spectacle. Skulls, arm and leg bones, hands and feet. There were at least three complete skeletons, and amidst the pale and pitted bones were feathers, clay beads, gnarled strips of leather. . . .

Jill picked up one of the leather strips and then put it down quickly, wiping her fingers on her pants. She couldn't be sure, but it felt like she imagined tanned, cured human skin would feel, stiff and kind of greasy—

Crash!

The window behind her exploded inward, a lithe, sinewy form lunging into the hall, growling and snapping. It was one of the mutant, killing hounds, its eyes as red as its dripping hide. It charged her, its teeth as bright and dangerous as the jagged glitter of glass still falling from the shattered frame.

Backed between two of the chests, Jill fired. The angle was wrong, the bullet splintering the wood at her feet as the dog jumped at her, growling deep in its throat.

It hit her in the thighs, slamming her painfully against the wall, gnashing to get its jaws at her flesh. The smell of rotting meat washed over her and she fired again and again, barely aware that she was moaning in fear and disgust, a sound as guttural and primal as the furious, dying shrieks that came from the canine abomination.

The fifth bullet fired directly into its barrel chest knocked it away. With a final, almost puppyish yelp it crumpled to the floor, blood gushing into the tan carpet.

Jill kept her weapon trained on the still form, gulping air in huge, shuddery breaths. Its limbs twitched suddenly, its massive claws beating a brief tattoo across the wet, red floor before it lay still again. Jill relaxed, recognizing the movement as a death spasm, the body releasing life. She'd have bruises, but the dog was dead.

She brushed her bangs out of her eyes and crouched down next to it, taking in the strange, exposed musculature and huge jaws. It had been too dark and hectic on the run to the house to get a good look at the things that had killed Joseph—but in the bright light of the corridor, her initial impression wasn't changed; it looked like a skinned dog.

She stood up and backed away, warily eyeing the row of windows in the hall. Obviously they offered no protection from the hazards outside. The corridor took a sharp left and she hurried on, past more of the macabre displays that decorated the inner wall.

The door at the end of the long hall was unlocked. It opened into another hall, not as well lit as the first but at least not as creepy, either. The muted, gray-green wallpaper sported paintings of generic scenery and gentle landscapes, not a bone or fetish in sight.

The first door on the right was locked, a carving of

armor on the key plate. Jill remembered the list on the computer, something about knight keys, but decided not to bother with it for now. According to Trent's map, there was a room on the other side that didn't lead anywhere. Besides, if Wesker *had* come this way, she didn't imagine that he was locking doors behind him. . . .

Right, just like it was unlikely that Chris would disappear; don't assume anything about this place.

The next door she tried opened into a small bathroom with an antique feel, complete with a ceiling fan and an old-fashioned, four-footed tub. There was no sign of recent use.

She stood for a moment in the stale, tiny room, breathing deeply, feeling the aftermath of the adrenaline rush she'd had in the corridor. Growing up, she'd learned how to enjoy the thrill of danger, of sneaking in and out of strange places with only a handful of tools and her own wits to keep her safe. Since joining the S.T.A.R.S., that youthful excitement had faded away, lost to the realities of back-up and handguns— but here it was again, unexpected and not unwelcome. She couldn't lie to herself about the simple joy that often followed facing death and walking away. She felt . . . *good.* Alive.

Let's not have a party just yet, her mind whispered sarcastically. *Or have you forgotten that S.T.A.R.S. are being eaten in this hellhole?*

Jill stepped back into the silent hallway and edged around another corner, wondering if Barry had found Chris and if either of them had run across any of the Bravos. She felt like she had an advantage with the maps, and decided that once she'd checked out the possible escape, she'd go back to the main hall and wait for Barry. With the information on Trent's computer, they could search more quickly and thoroughly.

The corridor ended with two doors facing each other. The one on the right was the one she wanted. She tried the handle and was rewarded with the soft *snick* of the bolt retracting.

She stepped into a dark hall and saw one of the zombies, a hulking, pale shadow standing next to a door, maybe ten feet away. As she raised her weapon, the creature started toward her, emitting soft hunger sounds from its decaying lips. One of its arms hung limply at its side, and although Jill could see jagged bone protruding from the shoulder, it still clenched and unclenched its rotting fist eagerly as it reached out with its other arm.

The head, aim for the head—

The shots were incredibly loud in the chilly gloom, the first blowing off its left ear, the second and third punching holes into its skull just above its pallid brow. Dark fluids streamed down the peeling face and it fell to its knees, its flat, lifeless eyes rolling back into its head.

There was shuffling movement in the shadows at the back of the hall to the right, exactly where she meant to go. Jill trained the gun on the darkness and waited for it to move closer, her entire body wired with tension.

How many of these things are there?

As soon as the zombie cleared the corner, she fired,

the Beretta jumping lightly in her sweating hands. The second shot punctured its right eye and it immediately collapsed to the dark, polished wood of the floor, the sticky, viscous matter of the blown eyeball flecked across its skeletal face.

Jill waited, but other than the spreading pools of blood around the dead creatures, nothing moved. Breathing through her mouth to avoid the worst of the stench, she hurried to the back of the hall and turned right, down a short, tight passage that dead ended at a rusting metal door.

It creaked open and fresh air flooded past her, warm and clean after the morgue-like chill of the house. Jill grinned, hearing the drone of cicadas and crickets on the night air. She'd reached the final leg of her little excursion, and although she wasn't outside yet, the sounds and smells of the forest renewed her sense of accomplishment.

Got a secured path now, straight to the back of this place. We can head north, hit one of the logging roads and hike down to the barricade. . . .

She stepped out onto a covered walkway, a mosaic of green stone surrounded by high concrete walls. There were small intermittent openings near the ceiling of the pathway, accounting for the faint, pine-scented breeze. Ivy trickled down from the arched openings like a reminder of the outside world. She hurried down the dim passage, remembering from the map that there was a single room at the end and to the right, probably a storage shed—

She turned the corner and stopped at another heavy-looking metal door, her smile fading as she reflexively reached for the handle; the keyhole was plugged. She crouched and poked at the tiny hole, but to no avail. Someone had stopped it up with epoxy.

To the left of the door was some kind of diagram set into the concrete, made of dull copper. There were four hexagonal depressions in the flat metal plate, each fist-sized hole connected to the next by a thin line. Jill squinted at the legend etched beneath, wishing that she had a flashlight as she struggled to make out the words. She brushed a thin layer of dust off of the indented letters and tried again.

WHEN THE SUN . . . SETS IN THE WEST AND THE MOON RISES IN THE EAST, STARS WILL BEGIN TO APPEAR IN THE SKY . . . AND WIND WILL BLOW TOWARD THE GROUND. THEN THE GATE OF NEW LIFE WILL OPEN.

She blinked. Four holes—

—*Trent's list! Four crests, and something about the gate of new life—it's a combination mechanism for the lock. Place the four crests, the door opens . . .*

. . . except that means I have to find *them first.*

Jill pushed against the door and felt her hope fizzle out completely; not even a rattle, no give at all. They were going to have to find another way out, unless the crests could be found—which in this place could take *years*.

A lone howl rose in the distance and was joined by the echoing cries of the dogs near the mansion, the strange, yodeling sounds piercing the gentle quiet of the woods. There had to be dozens of them out there, and Jill realized suddenly that escaping out the back door probably wasn't such a hot idea. She had limited ammunition for her handgun and no doubts that there were more ghoulish creatures wandering the halls, shuffling about in hungry, mindless silence as they searched for their next grisly meal. . . .

She sighed heavily and started back to the house, already dreading the cold stench of death and trying to prepare herself for the dangers that seemed to lurk at every corner.

The S.T.A.R.S. were trapped.

Chris knew he had to make the ammo count, so when he left Rebecca, he took off through the dim corridor at a full run, his boots pounding at the wood floor.

There were still only three of them, all grouped near the stairs. He dodged past them easily and sprinted down the hall and around the corner. As soon as he got to the door that led back to the other hall, he turned and assumed a classic shooter's stance, supporting his gun hand at the wrist, his finger on the trigger.

One by one, the zombies reeled around the corner, groaning and stumbling. Chris took careful aim, breathing evenly, keeping his focus. . . .

He squeezed the trigger, sending two bullets through the gangrenous nose of the first. Without pausing, he sent a third shot into the center of the next zombie's forehead. Fluid and soft matter sprayed the wall behind them as the bullets slapped into the wood.

Even as they crumpled to the floor, he'd found his mark on the third creature. Two more muted explosions and the zombie's brow caved inward, dropping it like the bag of bones that it was.

Chris lowered the Beretta, feeling a flush of pride. He was a high-ranked marksman, even had a couple of awards to show for it—but it was still good to see what he could do when given enough time to aim. His quick-draw wasn't nearly as strong, that was Barry's forte. . . .

He reached for the door handle, urged into action by the thought of all that was at stake. He figured the Alphas could take care of themselves, they had as much of a chance as he did—but this was Rebecca's first operation and she didn't even have a gun; he needed to get her out.

He stepped back into the soft light of the hall with the green wallpaper, quickly checking both directions. Straight ahead, the corridor was in heavier shadow; no way to tell if it was clear.

To his right was the door with the sword on the key plate and the first zombie he'd shot, still sprawled lifelessly across the floor. Chris was gratified to see that it hadn't moved. Apparently head shots *were* the best way to kill a zombie, just like in the movies. . . .

Chris edged toward the sword door, training his weapon left, then right, then left again; he'd had enough surprises for one day. He checked the small offshoot across from the door and seeing that it was clear, quickly inserted the slender key into the lock.

It turned smoothly. Chris stepped into a small bedroom, only slightly better lit than the corridor, a single bright lamp on a desk in one corner. It was all clear, unless there was something hiding under the narrow cot . . . or maybe in the closet across from the desk. . . .

He shuddered, closing the door behind him. It was every kid's first set of fears, and had been his, too— monsters in the closet and the thing that lived under the bed, waiting for the careless child's ankle to come within reach. . . .

And you're how *old now?*

Chris shook off the case of nerves, embarrassed at his imaginative wanderings. He walked slowly around the room, looking for anything that might be helpful. There was no other door, no path back to the main hall, but maybe he could find a better weapon for Rebecca than a can of bug spray.

Besides an oak table and bookshelf, there was the small, unmade bed and a study desk in the room, nothing more. He quickly rifled through the books, then moved around the foot of the bed to the desk. There was a slim volume next to the desk lamp, the fabric cover untitled; a journal. And although the desktop was coated in dust, the diary had been moved recently.

Intrigued, Chris picked it up and flipped to the last few pages. Maybe there was a clue as to what the hell was going on. He sat on the edge of the cot and started to read.

May 9, 1998: Played poker tonight with Scott and Alias from Security, and Steve from Research. Steve was the big winner, but I think he was cheating. Scumbag.

Chris smiled a little at that. He skipped down to the next entry and his smile froze, his heart seeming to pause in mid-beat.

May 10, 1998: One of the higher-ups assigned me to take care of a new experiment. It looks like a skinned gorilla. Feeding instructions were to give it live animals. When I threw in a pig, the creature seemed to be play with it . . tearing off the pig's legs and pulling out the guts before it actually started eating.

Experiment? Could the writer be talking about the zombies? Chris read on, excited by the find. The diary obviously belonged to someone who worked here, had to be—meaning that the cover-up was even bigger than he'd suspected.

May 11, 1998: At around 5 A.M., Scott woke me up. Scared the shit out of me, too. He was wearing a protective garment that looked like a space suit. He handed me another one and told me to put it on. Said there'd been an accident in the basement lab. I just knew something like this would happen. Those assholes in Research never rest, even at night.

May 12, 1998: I've been wearing the damn space suit since yesterday. My skin's getting grimy and feels itchy all over. The goddamn dogs have been looking at me funny, so I decided not to feed them today. Screw 'em.

May 13, 1998: Went to the Infirmary because my back is all swollen and feels itchy. They put a big bandage on it and told me I didn't need to wear the suit any more. All I wanna do is sleep.

May 14, 1998: Found another blister on my foot this

morning. I ended up dragging my foot all the way to the dogs' pen. They were quiet all day, which is weird. Then I realized some of them had escaped. If anybody finds out, I'll have my head handed to me.

May 15, 1998: My first day off in a long time and I feel like shit. Decided to go visit Nancy anyway, but when I tried to leave the estate, I was stopped by the guards. They said the company's ordered that no one leave the grounds. I can't even make a phone call—all the phones have been ripped out! What kind of bullshit is this?!

May 16, 1998: Rumor's going around that a researcher who tried to escape the estate last night was shot. My entire body feels hot and itchy and I'm sweating all the time now. I scratched the swelling on my arm and a piece of rotten flesh just dropped off. Wasn't until I realized the smell was making me hungry that I got violently sick.

The writing had become shaky. Chris turned the page, and could barely read the last few lines, the words scrawled haphazardly across the paper.

May 19. Fever gone but itchy. Hungry and eat doggie food. Itchy itchy Scott came ugly face so killed him. Tasty.

4 // Itchy. Tasty.

The rest of the pages were blank.

Chris stood up and slipped the journal inside his vest, his thoughts racing. Some of the pieces were finally fitting into place—secret research at a secretly kept estate, an accident in a hidden lab, an escaped virus or infection of some kind that altered the people working here, changing them into ghouls . . .

. . . and some of them got out.

The murders and attacks on Raccoon started in late May, coinciding with the effects of the "accident"; the chronology made sense. But exactly what kind of research was being done here, and how deeply involved was Umbrella?

How involved was Billy?

He didn't want to think about that—but even as he tried to clear his mind of the thought, a new one occurred to him . . . what if it was still contagious?

He hurried to the door, suddenly desperate to get back to Rebecca with the news. With her training, maybe she could figure out what had been unleashed in the secret lab on the estate.

Chris swallowed heavily. Even now, he and the other S.T.A.R.S. could be infected.

Eight

AFTER JILL AND BARRY WENT THEIR SEPA-
rate ways, Wesker stayed crouched on the balcony in
the main hall, thinking. He knew that time was of the
essence, but he wanted to outline a few possible
scenarios before he acted; he'd already made mistakes, and didn't want to make any more of them. The
Raccoon Alphas were a bright group, making his
margin for error very slim indeed.

He'd received his orders a couple of days ago, but
hadn't expected to be in a position to carry them out
so soon; the Bravo team's 'copter going down had
been a fluke, as had Brad Vickers's sudden display of
cowardice. Still, he should have been more prepared.
Being caught with his pants down like this went
against his grain, it was so . . . *unprofessional*.

He sighed, putting the thoughts aside. There'd be

time for self-recrimination later. He hadn't expected to end up here, but here he was, and kicking himself for lack of foresight wasn't going to change anything. Besides, there was too much to do.

He knew the grounds of the estate fairly well and the labs like the back of his hand, but he'd only been inside the mansion a few times—and not at all since he'd been "officially" transferred to Raccoon City. The place was a maze, designed by a genius architect at the bidding of a madman. Spencer was bats, no two ways about it, and he'd had the house built with all kinds of tricky little mechanisms, a lot of that silly spy crap that had been so popular in the late sixties. . . .

Spy crap that's going to make this job twice as hard as it needs to be. Hidden keys, secret tunnels—it's like I'm trapped in an espionage thriller, complete with mad scientists and a ticking clock. . . .

His original plan had been to lead both the Alpha and Bravo teams to the estate and clear the area before he proceeded to the lower labs and wrapped things up. He had the master keys and codes, of course; they had been sent along with his orders, and would open most of the doors on the estate. The problem was, there *was* no key to the door that led to the garden, it had a puzzle lock—and was currently the only way to get to the labs, outside of walking through the woods.

Which ain't gonna happen. The dogs would be on me before I could take two steps, and if the 121s got out . . .

Wesker shuddered, remembering the incident with the rookie guard who'd gotten too close to one of the cages, a year or so back. The kid had been dead before he could even open his mouth to call for help. Wesker had no intention of going back outside without an army to back him up.

The last contact with the estate had been over six weeks ago, an hysterical call from Michael Dees to one of the suits in the White office. The doctor had sealed the mansion, hiding the four pieces of the puzzle lock in a fruitless effort to keep any more of the virus carriers from reaching the house. By then, they were all infected and suffering from a kind of paranoid mania, one of the more charming side effects of the virus. God only knew what tricks and traps the researchers down in the labs had screwed with as they slowly lost their minds. . . .

Dees had been no exception, although he had managed to hold out longer than most of the others; something to do with individual metabolism, or so Wesker'd been told. The company had already decided to call a complete wipe, though the babbling scientist had been assured that help was on the way. Wesker had enjoyed a good laugh over *that* one. There was no way the White boys would risk further infection. They'd sat on their hands for almost two months while Raccoon suffered the consequences, letting the incompetent RPD investigate while the virus gradually lost its punch—and then sent him in to clean up the mess. Which by now was considerable.

The captain absently ran his fingers across the plush carpet, trying to remember details of the briefing about Dees's call. Whether he liked it or not, everything had to be taken care of tonight. He had to collect the required evidence and get to the labs, and that meant finding the pieces of the puzzle lock. Dees had been mostly incoherent, ranting about murderous crows and giant spiders—but he *had* insisted that the crest-keys to the puzzle lock were "hidden where only Spencer could find them," and that made sense. Everyone who worked in the house knew about Spencer's penchant for cloak-and-dagger mechanisms. Unfortunately for Wesker, he hadn't bothered learning much about the mansion, since he never thought he'd need the information. He remembered a few of the more colorful hiding places—the statue of the tiger with mismatched eyes came to mind, as did the armor display room with the gas and the secret room in the library. . . .

But I don't have time to go through all of them, not by myself. . . .

Wesker grinned suddenly and stood up, amazed that he hadn't thought of it already. Who said he had to be by himself? He'd ditched the S.T.A.R.S. to map out a new plan and search for the crests, but there was no reason that he had to do *everything*. Chris wasn't viable, he was too gung-ho, and Jill was still an unknown quantity . . . Barry, though . . . Barry Burton was a family man. And both Jill and Chris trusted him.

And while they're all still fumbling around in the house, I can get to the triggering system and then get the hell out, mission complete.

Still grinning, Wesker walked to the door that led to the dining room balcony, surprised to find that he was looking forward to his little adventure. It was a chance to test his skills against the rest of the team and against the accidental test subjects that were surely still lurching around—not to mention, ol' Spencer himself. And if he pulled it off, he was going to be a very rich man.

This might actually turn out to be fun.

Πίπε

CAW!

Jill whipped her Beretta toward the sound, the mournful shriek echoing all around as the door slipped closed behind her. Then she saw the source of the noise and relaxed, smiling nervously.

What the hell are they *doing in here?*

She was still in the back part of the house, and had decided to check out a few of the other rooms before heading back to the main hall. The first door she'd tried had been locked, a carving of a helmet on the key plate. Her picks had been useless, the lock a type she'd never encountered, so she'd decided to try her luck on the door across the hall. It had opened easily enough, and she'd gone in ready for anything—though about the last thing she'd expected to see was a flock of crows, perched along the support bar for the track lighting that ran the length of the room.

Another of the large black birds let out its morose shriek, and Jill shivered at the sound. There were at least a dozen of them, ruffling their shiny feathers and watching her with bright, beady eyes as she quickly surveyed the room for threats; it was clear.

The U-shaped chamber she'd entered was as cold as the rest of the house, perhaps colder, and empty of furniture. It was a viewing hall, nothing but portraits and paintings lining the inner wall. Black feathers lay scattered across the worn wooden floor amidst dried mounds of bird droppings, and Jill wondered again how the crows had gotten inside, and how long they'd been there. There was definitely something strange about their appearance; they seemed much larger than normal crows, and they studied her with an intensity that seemed almost—*unnatural.*

Jill shivered again, turning back toward the door. There wasn't anything important in the room, and the birds were giving her the creeps. Time to move on.

She glanced at a few of the paintings on her way out, mostly portraits, noticing that there were switches beneath the heavy frames—she assumed they were for the track lighting, though she couldn't imagine why anyone had bothered setting up such an elaborate gallery for such mediocre art. A baby, a young man . . . the paintings weren't awful, but they weren't exactly inspired, either.

She stopped as she touched the cold metal handle of the door, frowning. There was a small, inset control panel set at eye level to the right of the door, labeled "spots." She punched one of the buttons and the room dimmed as a single directional light went out. Several of the crows barked their disapproval, fluttering ebony wings, and Jill turned the light back on, thinking.

So if these are the light switches, what are the controls beneath the paintings for?

Perhaps there was more to the room than she'd thought. She walked to the first picture across from the door, a large painting of flying angels and clouds shot with sunbeams. The title was, *From Cradle to Grave.* There wasn't a switch below it, and Jill moved to the next.

It was a portrait of a middle-aged man, his lined features sagging with exhaustion, standing next to an elaborate fireplace. From the cut of his suit and his slicked back hair, it looked to have been painted in the late 1940s or early '50s. There was a simple on/off switch underneath, unlabeled. Jill flicked it from left to right and heard an electrical *snap*—

—and behind her, the crows exploded into screaming motion, rising as one from their brooding perch. All she could hear was the beat of their dark wings and the sudden, manic ferocity of their cries as they swarmed toward her—

—and Jill ran, the door seeming a million miles away, her heart pounding. The first of the crows reached her as she grabbed for the handle, its claws finding the soft skin at the back of her neck. There was a sharp stab of pain just behind her right ear and Jill flailed at the rustling feathers that brushed her cheeks, moaning as the furious shrieks enveloped her. She slapped at the air behind her and was rewarded with a startled *squawk* of surprise. The bird let go of her, reeling away.

—too many, out out OUT—

She jerked the door open and fell into the hallway, kicking the door closed even as she hit the floor. She lay there a moment, catching her breath, relishing the cool silence of the corridor in spite of the zombie stench. None of the crows had gotten out.

As her heartbeat returned to something approaching normal, she sat up and carefully touched the wound behind her ear. Her fingers came away wet, but it wasn't too bad, the blood was already clotting; she'd been lucky. When she thought of what could have happened if she'd tripped and fallen . . .

Why had they attacked, what had the control switch done? She remembered the snap of electricity when she'd flipped it, the sound of a spark—

—the perch!

She felt a sudden rush of grudging admiration for whoever had set up the simple trap. When she'd hit the switch, she must have sent a current through the metal bar they'd been perched on. She'd never heard of attack-trained crows, but could think of no other explanation—which meant that someone had gone through a lot of trouble to keep whatever was in that room a secret. To get to the answer, she'd have to go back in.

I can stand in the doorway, take them out one at a

time. . . . She didn't much like the idea, she didn't trust her aim and would certainly waste a lot of ammunition.

Only fools accept the obvious and go no further; use your brain, Jilly.

Jill smiled a little; it was her father talking, reminding her of the training she'd had before the S.T.A.R.S. One of her earliest memories was of hiding in the bushes outside the rickety old house in Massachusetts that her father had rented for them, studying the dark, empty windows as he explained how to properly "case a prospect." Dick had made it into a game, teaching her over the next ten years all the finer points of breaking and entering, everything from how to remove panes of glass without damaging them to walking on stairs so they didn't creak—and he'd also taught her, again and again, that every riddle had more than one answer.

Killing the birds was too obvious. She closed her eyes, concentrating.

Switches and portraits . . . a little boy, a toddler, a young man, a middle-aged man . . .

"From Cradle to Grave." *Cradle to grave . . .*

Once the solution occurred to her, she was almost embarrassed by the simplicity of it. She stood up and dusted herself off, wondering how long it would take for the crows to return to their roost. Once they were settled, she shouldn't have any more problems uncovering the secret.

She cracked the door open and listened to the whispering beat of wings, promising herself to be more careful this time. Pushing the wrong button in this house could be deadly.

"Rebecca? Let me in, it's Chris."

There was the sound of something heavy sliding against the wall and the door to the storage room creaked opened. Rebecca stepped away from the entrance as he hurried inside, already pulling the diary out of his vest.

"I found this journal in one of the rooms," he said. "It looks like there was some kind of research going on here, I don't know what kind but—"

"Virology," Rebecca interrupted, and held up a stack of papers, grinning. "You were right about there being something useful in here."

Chris took the papers from her and skimmed the first page. As far as he could tell, it was in a foreign language made out of numbers and letters.

"What is all this stuff? DH5a-MCR . . ."

"You're looking at a strain chart," Rebecca said brightly. "That one's a host for generating genomic libraries containing methylated cytosine—or adenine residues, depending."

Chris cocked an eyebrow at her. "Let's pretend that I have no idea what you're talking about and try again. What did you find?"

Rebecca flushed slightly and took the papers back from him. "Sorry. Basically, there's a lot of, uh, *stuff* in here on viral infection."

Chris nodded. "That I understand; a virus . . ."

He quickly flipped through the journal, counting the dates from the first report of the accident in the lab. "On May eleventh, there was some kind of spill or outbreak in a laboratory on this estate. Within eight or nine days, whoever wrote this had turned into one of those creatures out there."

Rebecca's eyes widened. "Does it say when the first symptoms appeared?"

"Looks like . . . within twenty-four hours, he or she was complaining of itchy skin. Swelling and blisters within forty-eight hours."

Rebecca paled. "That's . . . wow."

Chris nodded. "Yeah, my thoughts exactly. Is there any way to tell if we could be infected?"

"Not without more information. All of that—" Rebecca motioned at the trunk full of papers, "—is pretty old, ten years plus, and there's nothing specific about application. Though an airborne with that kind of speed and toxicity . . . if it was still viable, all of Raccoon City would probably be infected by now. I can't be positive, but I doubt it's still contagious."

Chris was relieved for himself and the rest of the S.T.A.R.S., but the fact that the "zombies" were all victims of a disease—it was depressing, whether it was a disaster of their own making or not.

"We have to find the others," he said. "If one of them should stumble across the lab without knowing what's there . . ."

Rebecca looked stricken at the thought, but nodded gamely and moved quickly toward the door. Chris decided that, with a little experience, she'd make a first-rate S.T.A.R.S. member; she obviously knew her chemistry, and even without a gun, she was willing to leave the relative safety of the storage room in order to help the rest of the team.

Together, they hurried through the dark, wooded hallway, Rebecca sticking close to his side. When they reached the door back to the first hallway, Chris checked his Beretta and then turned to Rebecca.

"Stay close. The door we want is to the right and at the end of the hall. I'll probably have to shoot the lock, and I'm pretty sure there's a zombie or two wandering around, so I'll need you to watch my back."

"Yes, sir," she said quietly, and Chris grinned in spite of the situation. Technically, he *was* her superior—still, it was weird to have it pointed out.

He opened the door and stepped through, training his gun on the shadows straight ahead and then down the hall to the right. Nothing moved.

"Go," he whispered, and they jogged down the corridor, quickly stepping over the fallen creature that blocked their path. Rebecca turned to face the open stretch behind them as Chris rattled the door knob, hoping vainly that it had unlocked itself.

No such luck. He backed away from the door and took careful aim. Firing at a locked door wasn't as easy or safe as it looked in the movies; a ricochet off of metal at such close range could kill the shooter—

"Chris!"

He glanced over his shoulder and saw a shambling figure at the other end of the hall, moving slowly toward them. Even in the dim light, Chris could see that one of its arms was missing. The distinctive odor of decay wafted toward them as the zombie moaned thickly, stumbling forward.

Chris turned back to the door and fired, twice. The frame splintered, the inset metal square of the lock revealed in a spray of wood chips. He jerked at the knob and the lock gave, the door swinging open.

He turned and grabbed at Rebecca's arm, hustling her through the doorway as he pointed the Beretta back down the hall. The creature had made it halfway, but was stopped at the lifeless body of the zombie that Chris had killed earlier. Even as Chris watched in horror and disgust, the one-armed zombie dropped to its knees and plunged its remaining hand into the other's crushed skull. It moaned again, a wet, phlegmy sound, and brought a handful of slushy gray matter to its eager lips.

Oh, man—

Chris shuddered involuntarily and hurriedly stepped through to join Rebecca, closing the door on the gruesome scene. Rebecca was pale but seemed composed, and again, Chris admired her courage; she was young but tough, tougher than he'd been at eighteen. . . .

He took in the hall at a glance, immediately noticing the changes. To their right about twenty feet away was a corpse of one of the creatures, the top of its head blown away. It lay face up, the deep sockets of its eyes filled with blood. To their left were the two doors that Chris hadn't tried when he'd first come to investigate. The one at the very end of the hall was standing open, revealing deep shadows.

At least one of the S.T.A.R.S. came this way, probably looking for me. . . .

"Follow me," he said softly, and moved toward the open door, holding the Beretta tightly. He wanted to get back to the main hall with Rebecca, but the fact that one of his team must have gone through the opening deserved a quick look.

As they passed the closed door on the right, Rebecca hesitated. "There's a picture of a sword next to the lock," she whispered.

He kept his attention on the darkness just past the open door, but realized as she spoke that there were too many ways for them to get side-tracked. He didn't think the rest of the team was still waiting for him, but his original orders had been to report back to the lobby; he shouldn't be leading an unarmed rookie into unknown territory without at least checking.

Chris sighed, lowering his weapon. "Let's get back to the main hall," he said. "We can come back and check it out later."

Rebecca nodded and together they walked back toward the dining room, Chris hoping against hope that someone would be there to meet them.

Barry pointed his Colt toward the crawling ghoul and fired, the heavy round splattering the thing's mushy skull into liquid even as it reached for his boot. Tiny drops of wetness splashed his face as the zombie spasmed and died. Scowling, Barry wiped at his skin with the back of his hand. The tiny white tiles of the kitchen wall got it much worse, rivulets of red coursing down the grouted tracks and pooling to the faded brown linoleum. Still, it was pretty disgusting.

Barry lowered the revolver, feeling the ache in his left shoulder. The door upstairs had been solidly locked, he had the bruises to prove it—and staring down at the zombie hash in front of him, he realized that he was going to have to go back up and break down another one. If he hadn't been certain before, he was now—Chris hadn't come this way. If he had, the crawling creature would already have been history.

So where the hell are you, Chris?

Of the three locked doors, Barry had picked the one at the end of the hall on pure instinct. He'd ended up in a dark, silent hall that led past an empty elevator shaft and down a narrow set of stairs. The bare white kitchen at the bottom had seemed deserted, the counters thick with dust and corrosion stains on the walls—no sign of recent use, no sign of Chris, and the single door across from the sink had been locked. He'd been about to leave when he'd noticed the trails of disturbed dust on the floor and followed them. . . .

Sighing heavily, Barry stepped over the stinking monster, a final check before he headed back up for door number two. There were some stacked crates and the same old-fashioned elevator shaft, also empty. He didn't bother with the call button since the one upstairs hadn't worked. Besides, judging from the rust on the metal grate, no one had used it in quite awhile.

He turned back the way he'd come, wondering how Jill was making out. The sooner they could get away, the better. Barry had never disliked any place as much as he did this mansion. It was cold, it was dangerous, and it smelled like a meat locker that had been unplugged for a week. He generally wasn't the type to frighten easily or let his imagination get out of hand, but he half-expected to see some white-sheeted spook rattling chains every time he turned around—

There was a distant echoing clatter behind him. Barry spun, a knot of dread in his gut as he pointed his weapon randomly at the empty air, his eyes wide and mouth dry. There was another metallic clatter, followed by a low, throbbing hum of machinery.

Barry took a deep breath and blew it out slowly, getting a hold of himself. Not a disembodied spirit, after all; someone was using the elevator.

Who? Chris and Wesker are missing and Jill's in the other wing. . . .

He stayed where he was, lowering the Colt slightly as he waited. He didn't think the ghouls were smart enough to work the buttons, let alone open the gate, but he didn't want to take any chances. He was a good twenty feet from where the booth would open, assuming it stopped in the basement, and would have a clear shot at whoever stepped around the corner. A glimmer of hope sparked through his confusion; maybe it was one of the Bravos, or someone who lived here and could tell them what had happened. . . .

With a dull *clang,* the elevator stopped in the kitchen. There was a squeal of dry metal hinges and footsteps—

—and Captain Wesker stepped into view, his perpetual sunglasses propped on his tanned brow.

Barry lowered the revolver, grinning as cool relief

swept over him. Wesker stopped in his tracks and grinned back at him.

"Barry! Just the man I was looking for," he said lightly.

"God, you gave me a scare! I heard the elevator start up and thought I was gonna have a heart attack . . ." Barry trailed off, his grin faltering.

"Captain," he said slowly, "where did you go? When we came back, you were gone."

Wesker's grin widened. "Sorry about that. I had some business to attend to—you know, call of nature?"

Barry smiled again, but was surprised by the confession; trapped in hostile territory, and the man had gone off to take a leak?

Wesker reached up and lowered his shades, breaking their eye contact, and Barry suddenly felt a little nervous. Wesker's grin, if anything, seemed to grow wider. It looked like every tooth was showing.

"Barry, I need your help. Have you ever heard of White Umbrella?"

Barry shook his head, feeling more uncomfortable by the second.

"White Umbrella is a sector of Umbrella, Inc., a very important division. They specialize in . . . biological research, I guess you could say. The Spencer estate houses their research facilities, and recently, an accident occurred."

Wesker brushed off a section of the kitchen's center island and casually leaned against it, his tone almost conversational.

"This division of Umbrella has a few ties to the S.T.A.R.S. organization, and not long ago, I was asked to . . . *assist* in their handling of this situation. It's a very delicate situation, mind you, very hush-hush; White Umbrella doesn't want a whisper of their involvement getting out.

"Now, what *I'm* supposed to do is get to the laboratories on the grounds here and put an end to some rather incriminating evidence—proof that White Umbrella is responsible for the accident that's caused so much trouble in Raccoon as of late. The problem is, I don't have the key to get to those labs—keys, actually. And that's where you come in. I need for you to help me find those keys."

Barry stared at him for a moment, speechless, his mind churning. An accident, a secret lab doing biological research . . .

. . . *and murdering dogs and zombies loose in the woods* . . .

He raised his revolver and pointed it at Wesker's smiling face, stunned and angry. "Are you *insane?* You think I'm going to help you destroy evidence? You crazy son of a bitch!"

Wesker shook his head slowly, acting as if Barry were a child. "Ah, Barry, you don't understand; you don't have a choice in the matter. See, a few of my friends from White Umbrella are currently standing outside of your house, watching your wife and daughters sleep. If you *don't* help me, your family is going to die."

Barry could actually feel the blood drain from his

face. He cocked the hammer back on the Colt, feeling a sudden, vicious hatred for Wesker infusing every fiber of his being.

"Before you pull the trigger, I should mention that if I don't report back to my friends fairly soon, their orders are to go ahead and do the deed anyway."

The words cut through the red haze that had flooded Barry's mind, turning his hands clammy with terror.

Kathy, the babies—!

"You're bluffing," he whispered, and Wesker's grin finally disappeared, his expression slipping back into the unreadable mask that he usually wore.

"I'm not," he said coldly. "Try me. You can apologize to their headstones later."

For a moment, neither of them moved, the silence a palpable thing in the chill air. Then Barry slowly eased the hammer back down and lowered the weapon, his shoulders slumped. He couldn't, *wouldn't* risk it; his family was everything.

Wesker nodded and reached into one of his pockets, producing a ring of keys, his manner suddenly brisk and business-like. "There are four copper plates somewhere in this house. Each one is about the size of a teacup, and has a picture engraved on one side— sun, moon, stars, and wind. There's a back door on the other side of the mansion where the four of them belong."

He unhooked a key from the ring and set it on the table, sliding it across to Barry. "This should open all of the doors in the other wing, or at least the important ones, first and second floor. Find those pieces for me and your wife and children will be fine."

Barry reached for the key with numb fingers, feeling weak and more afraid than he'd ever been in his life. "Chris and Jill . . ."

". . . will undoubtedly want to help you search. If you see either of them, tell them that the back door you've discovered could be the way out. I'm sure they'll be more than happy to work with their trusted friend, good ol' Barry. In fact, you should unlock every door you can in order to promote a more thorough job."

Wesker smiled again, a friendly half-grin that belied his words. "Of course, you tell them you've seen me—that could complicate matters. If I run into trouble, say, get shot in the back . . . well, enough said. Let's just keep this to ourselves."

The key was etched with a little picture, a chest plate for a suit of armor. Barry slipped it into his pocket. "Where will you be?"

"Oh, I'll be around, don't worry. I'll contact you when the time is right."

Barry looked at Wesker pleadingly, helpless to keep the wavering fear out of his voice. "You'll tell them that I'm helping you, right? You won't forget to report?"

Wesker turned and walked toward the elevator, calling out over his shoulder. "Trust me, Barry. Do what I tell you, and there's nothing to worry about."

There was the rattle of the elevator's gate opening and closing, and Wesker was gone.

Barry stood a moment longer, staring into the empty space where Wesker had been, trying to find a way out of the threat. There wasn't one. There was no contest between his honor and his family; he could live without honor.

He set his jaw and walked back toward the stairs, determined to do what he had to do to save Kathy and the girls. Though when this was over, when he could be sure they were safe—

There won't be any place for you to hide, "Captain."

Barry clenched his giant fists, knuckles whitening, and promised himself that Wesker would pay for what he was doing. With interest.

†ᴇɴ

JILL SLID THE HEAVY COPPER CREST WITH the engraved star into its position on the diagram, above the other three openings. It settled into place with a light *click,* flush against the metal plate.

One down . . . She stepped back from the puzzle lock, smiling triumphantly.

The crows had watched her walk through the hall of paintings without moving from their perch, crying out occasionally as she solved the simple puzzle. There had been six portraits in all, cradle to grave— from a newborn baby to a rather stern-looking old man. She'd assumed they were all of Lord Spencer, though she'd never seen a photo. . . .

The final painting had been a death scene, a pale man lying in state and surrounded by mourners. When she'd flipped the switch on that one, the painting had actually fallen off the wall, pushed out by tiny metal pegs at each corner. Behind it had been a small, velvet-lined opening that held the copper crest. She'd left the hall without any more trouble; if the birds had been disappointed, she couldn't say.

She took a final deep breath of the pleasant night air before going back into the mansion, pulling Trent's computer from her pack as she went. Stepping carefully over the crumpled corpse in the dim hall, she studied the map, deciding where to try next.

Back the way she'd come, it looked like. She went back through the double doors that connected the corridors, into the winding, mild, gray-green hall with the landscape paintings. According to the map, the single door just across from her led to a small, square-shaped room which opened into a larger one.

Tensing, she grabbed the knob and pushed it open, crouching and pointing her Beretta at the same time. The small room was indeed square-shaped, and totally empty.

Straightening, Jill stepped into the chamber, briefly appraising its simple elegance as she walked toward the door on her right. It had a high, light ceiling and the walls were creamy marble flecked with gold; beautiful. And expensive, to say the least. She felt a vague wistfulness for the old days with Dick, all their grand plans and hopes for each score. This was what *real* money could buy. . . .

She readied herself, grasping the cold, flowing metal of the latch and pushing the door open. A quick sweep with the Beretta and she felt herself relax; she was alone.

There was a molded fireplace to her right beneath an ornate, red and gold tapestry. A low, modern couch and oval coffee table sat atop a burnt orange carpet of oriental design, and against the back wall—

—a pump-action shotgun was mounted on dual hooks, shining in the light from the antique light fixture overhead. Jill grinned and hurried across the room, unable to believe her luck.

Please be loaded, please be loaded—

As she stopped in front of it, she recognized the make. Guns weren't her strong suit, but it was the same as the S.T.A.R.S. used: a Remington M870, five shots.

She holstered the Beretta and lifted the shotgun with both hands, still grinning—

—and the smile dropped away as both mounting hooks clicked upward, released from the weight of the gun. At the same time, there was a heavier sound behind the wall, a sound like balanced metal changing position.

Jill didn't know what it was, but she didn't like it. She turned around quickly, searching the room for movement. It was as still as when she'd entered, no screaming birds, no sudden alarms or flashing lights, none of the pictures fell off the wall. There was no trap.

Relieved, she quickly checked the weapon and found it fully loaded. Someone had taken care of it, the barrel clean and smelling faintly of cleaner and oil; right now, it was about the best smell she could imagine. The solid weight of it in her hands was reassuring, the weight of power.

She searched the rest of the room and was disappointed not to find any more shells. Still, the Remington was a find. S.T.A.R.S. vests had a back holster for a shotgun or rifle, and although she wasn't that hot with an over-the-shoulder draw, at least she could carry it without tying up her hands.

There was nothing else of interest in the room. Jill walked to the door, excited to get back to the main hall and share her discoveries with Barry. She'd checked out every room that she could open on this side of the first floor. If he'd managed the same, they could head upstairs to finish their search for the Bravos and their missing teammates—

And then, hopefully, get the hell out of this morgue.

She closed the door behind her and strode across the slate-colored tiles of the classy marble room, hoping, as she grasped the knob, that Barry had found Chris and Wesker. *They sure didn't come this way—*

The door was locked. Jill frowned, turning the small gold knob back and forth. It rattled a little, but wouldn't give at all. She peered at the crack where the door met the frame, suddenly a little anxious.

There it was, by the handle—the thick sliver of steel that indicated a dead-bolt, and a very solid one; the entire area surrounding it was reinforced. *But only one keyhole, and that's for the knob—*

Click! Click! Click!

Dust rained down from above as the sound of gears

turning filled the room, a deep, rhythmic clatter of metal from somewhere behind the stone walls.

What—?

Startled, Jill looked up—and felt her stomach shrivel in on itself, her breath catching in her throat. The high ceiling that she'd admired earlier was moving, the marble at the corners powdering into dust with the heavy grind of stone against stone. It was coming down.

In a flash she was back at the door to the shotgun room. She snatched at the handle, pushing it down . . .

. . . and found it locked as solidly as the first.

Holy shit! Bad thing! Bad thing!

Panic rising through her system, Jill ran back to the other door, her frightened gaze drawn back to the lowering ceiling. At two to three inches each second, it'd hit the floor in less than a minute.

Jill raised the shotgun and aimed at the door to the hall, trying not to think about how many shots it would take to blow apart a reinforced steel dead-bolt; it was all she had, the picks wouldn't work on that kind of lock—

The first round exploded against the door and splinters flew, revealing exactly what she'd feared. The metal plate that supported the bolt extended across half the door. Her mind raced for an answer and came up blank. She didn't have the shells to blow through it and the Beretta carried hollow points, they flattened on impact.

Maybe I can weaken it, break it down—

She fired again, targeting the frame itself. The thunderous shot tore apart wood and chipped marble, but not enough, not even close. The ceiling continued its clattering descent, now less than ten feet above her head. She was going to be crushed to death.

God, don't let me die like this—

"Jill? Is that you?"

A muffled voice called from the corridor, and she felt a sudden, desperate hope course through her at the sound.

Barry!

"Help! Barry, break it down, now!" Jill shouted, her voice high and shaking.

"Get back!"

Jill stumbled away as she heard a heavy blow strike the door. The wood shuddered but held. Jill let out a low cry of helpless frustration, her terrified gaze jumping between the door and the ceiling.

Another solid, shaking hit to the door. Five feet overhead.

Come on, come ON—

The third pounding blow was joined by the crunch and splinter of wood. The door flew open, Barry framed in the entry, his face red and sweating, his hand reaching for hers.

Jill lunged forward and he grabbed her wrist, literally jerking her off of her feet and into the corridor. They crashed to the floor as behind them, the door was crushed off its hinges. Wood and metal squealed as the ceiling continued smoothly down, the door snapping in a series of harsh *cracks*.

With a final, resonating *boom* of impact, the ceiling

met the floor. It was over, the house again as silent as a tomb. They staggered to their feet, Jill staring at the doorway. The entire frame was filled with the solid block of stone that had been the ceiling, at least a couple of tons of rock.

"Are you alright?" Barry asked.

Jill didn't answer for a moment. She looked down at the shotgun she still held in her trembling hands, remembering how confident she'd been that there'd been no trap—and for the first time, she wondered how they were ever going to make it out of this hellish place.

They stood in the empty front hall, Chris pacing the carpet in front of the stairs, Rebecca standing nervously by the banister. The massive lobby was as cold and ominous as when Chris had first seen it, the mute walls giving away none of their secrets; the S.T.A.R.S. were gone, and there were no clues as to where or why.

From somewhere deep in the mansion, there was a heavy rumbling sound, like a giant door being slammed. They both cocked their heads, listening, but it wasn't repeated. Chris couldn't even tell from what direction it had come.

Terrific, that's just great. Zombies, mad scientists, and now things that go bump in the night. Priceless.

He smiled at Rebecca, hoping that he looked less rattled than he felt. "Well, no forwarding message. I guess that moves us to plan B."

"What's plan B?"

Chris sighed. "Hell if I know. But we can start by checking out that other room with the sword key.

Maybe we can dig up some more information while we wait for the team to reassemble, a map or something."

Rebecca nodded, and they headed back through the dining room, Chris leading the way. He didn't like the idea of exposing her to further danger, but he didn't want to leave her alone, either, at least not in the main hall; it didn't feel safe.

As they passed the ticking grandfather clock, something small and hard cracked beneath Chris's boot. He crouched down and scooped up a dark gray chunk of plaster. There were two or three other fragments nearby.

"Did you notice these when we came through before?" he asked.

Rebecca shook her head, and Chris ducked down, looking for more of them. He didn't remember if they'd been there before, either. On the other side of the table was a broken pile of the fragments.

They hurried around the end of the long table past the elaborately decorated fireplace, stopping in front of the shattered pile. Chris nudged at the gray pieces with the tip of his boot. From the angles and shapes, it appeared to have been a statue of some kind.

Whatever it was, *it's garbage now.*

"Is it important?" Rebecca asked.

Chris shrugged. "Maybe, maybe not. Worth a look, anyway. In a situation like this, you never know what might turn out to be a clue."

The echoing tick of the old clock followed them back to the hall door and into the smell of decay that filled the tight corridor. Chris pulled the silver key out of a pocket as they headed right—

—and stopped, quickly drawing his Beretta and moving closer to Rebecca. The door at the end of the hall was closed; when they'd left, it had been standing open.

There was no sense of being watched, of movement in the hall, but someone must have come through while they'd been in the lobby. The thought was disconcerting, reaffirming Chris's uneasy feeling that secret things were happening all around them. The dead creature to their left was in the same position as before, its blood-filled eyes staring blindly at the low ceiling, and Chris wondered again who had killed it. He knew he should examine the corpse and the unsecured area beyond it, but didn't want to go off on his own until he got Rebecca somewhere safe.

"Come on," he whispered, and they edged to the locked door, Chris handing the key to Rebecca so that he could watch the hall for attackers. With a soft *click,* the intricately paneled door was unlocked, and Rebecca gently pushed it open.

Chris could feel that the room was okay even as he did a quick check and motioned for Rebecca to step inside. It was set up like a piano bar, a baby grand dominating the floor across from a built-in counter, complete with stools bolted along its length. Perhaps it was the soft lighting or the muted colors that gave it such an atmosphere of calm stillness. Whatever it was, Chris decided that it was the nicest room he'd encountered so far.

And maybe a good place for Rebecca to stay while I try to find the others. . . .

Rebecca perched herself on the edge of the dusty black piano bench while Chris did a more thorough search of the room. There were a couple of potted plants, a small table, and a tiny alcove behind the wall where the piano was situated, a couple of wood bookshelves pushed in back. The only entrance was the one they'd come through. It was an ideal spot for Rebecca to hide.

He holstered his weapon and joined her at the piano, trying to choose his words carefully; he didn't want to scare her with the suggestion that she stay behind. She smiled up at him hesitantly, looking even younger than she was, her spiky red bangs adding to the impression that she was only a child. . . .

. . . A child who got through college in less time than it took you to get your pilot's license; don't patronize her, she's probably smarter than you *are.*

Chris sighed inwardly and smiled back at her. "How would you feel about staying here while I take a look around the house?"

Her smile faltered a little, but she met his gaze evenly. "Makes sense," she said. "I don't have a gun, and if you run into trouble, I'd just slow you down. . . ."

She grinned wider and added, "Though if you get your ass kicked by a mathematical theorem, don't come crying to me."

Chris laughed, as much at his own faulty assumptions as at her joke; she wasn't one to be underestimated. He walked to the door, pausing as his hand touched the knob.

"I'll be back as soon as I can," he said. "Lock the door behind me, and don't go wandering off, okay?"

Rebecca nodded, and he stepped back into the hall, closing the door firmly behind him. He waited until he heard the bolt drawn and drew his Beretta, the last trace of a smile falling away as he started briskly down the corridor.

The closer he got to the rotting creature, the worse the smell. He took shallow sips of air as he reached the body, stepping past it to see if the hall continued on before he examined it for bullet holes—

—and he stopped cold, staring at the second corpse stretched out in the alcove, headless and covered in blood. Chris studied the slack, lifeless features of the face that lay a foot away, recognizing them as Kenneth Sullivan's—and felt a surge of anger and renewed determination sweep through him at the sight of the dead Bravo.

This is wrong, all wrong. Joseph, Ken, probably Billy—how many others have died? How many more have to suffer because of a stupid accident?

He finally turned away, striding purposefully toward the door that led back to the dining room. He'd start from the main hall, checking every possible path that the S.T.A.R.S. could have taken and killing every creature that got in the way of his search.

His teammates weren't going to have died for nothing; Chris would see to it, if it was the last thing he ever did.

Rebecca locked the door after Chris left, silently wishing him good luck before walking back to the dusty piano and sitting down. She knew that he felt responsible for her, and wondered again how she could've been so stupid, dropping her gun.

At least if I had a gun, he wouldn't have to worry so much. I may be inexperienced, but I went through basic training, just like everybody else. . . .

She traced a finger aimlessly across the dusty keys, feeling useless. She should've taken some of those files from the storage room. She didn't know that there was much more to be learned from them, but at least she'd have something to read. She wasn't very good at sitting still, and having nothing to do only made it worse.

You could practice, her mind suggested brightly, and Rebecca smiled a little, gazing down at the keys. *No, thanks.* She'd suffered through four long years of lessons as a child before her mother had finally let her quit.

She stood up, looking randomly around the silent room for something to keep her occupied. She walked to the bar and leaned over it, but saw only a few shelves of glasses and a stack of napkins, all thinly coated with dust. There were several liquor bottles, most of them empty, and a few unopened bottles of expensive-looking wine on the counter behind the bar. . . .

Rebecca dismissed the thought even as it occurred to her. She wasn't much of a drinker, and now wasn't exactly the best time to tie one on. Sighing, she turned and surveyed the rest of the room.

Besides the piano, there wasn't much to see. There was a single small painting of a woman on the wall to her left, a bland portrait in a dark frame; a slowly dying plant on the floor next to the piano, the leafy kind she always saw in nice restaurants; a table that extended out from the wall with an overturned martini glass on top. Considering what she had to work with, the piano was starting to look pretty interesting. . . .

She walked past the baby grand and peered into the small opening to her right. There were two empty bookshelves pushed to one side, nothing interesting—

Frowning, she stepped closer to the shelves. The smaller one on the outside was empty, but the one behind it—

She placed her hands on either side of the end piece and pushed, sliding the outer shelf forward. It wasn't heavy and moved easily, leaving a track in the dust on the wood floor.

Rebecca scanned the hidden shelves, feeling disappointed. A dented old bugle, a dusty glass candy dish, a couple of knickknack vases—and some piano sheet music propped up on a tiny holder. She peered down at the title and felt a sudden rush of warm nostalgia for when she used to play; it was *Moonlight Sonata,* one of her favorite pieces.

She picked up the yellowing sheets, remembering the hours she'd put in trying to learn it when she was ten or eleven. In fact, it had been this very piece of music that had made her realize she wasn't cut out to be a pianist. It was a beautiful, delicate tune and she'd pretty much butchered it every time she took the bench.

Still holding the composition, she walked back around the corner and gazed at the piano thoughtfully. It wasn't like she had anything better to do. . . .

And besides, maybe one of the other team members will hear it and come knocking, trying to track down the source of the terrible noise.

Grinning, she dusted the bench off and sat down, propping the sheets open on the music holder. Her fingers found the correct positions almost automatically as she read the opening notes, like she'd never given it up. It was a comforting feeling, a welcome change from the horrors inside the mansion.

Slowly, hesitantly, she started to play. As the first melancholy sounds rose into the stillness, Rebecca found herself relaxing, letting tension and fear slip away. She still wasn't very good, her tempo as off as ever—but she hit all the right notes, and the strength of the melody more than made up for her lack of finesse.

If only the keys weren't so stiff—

Something moved behind her.

Rebecca jumped up, knocking the bench over as she spun around, searching wildly for the attacker. What she saw was so unexpected that she froze for a few seconds, unable to comprehend what her senses were telling her.

The wall *is moving—*

Even as the last notes lingered in the cool air, a three-foot panel of the bare wall to her right slid upwards into the ceiling, rumbling to a gentle halt.

For a moment she didn't move, waiting for something terrible to happen—but as the seconds ticked past in silence, nothing else moved; the room was as quiet and non-threatening as before.

Hidden sheet music. A strange stiffness to the keys . . .

. . . *like maybe they were connected to some kind of a mechanism?*

The narrow opening revealed a hidden chamber about the size of a walk-in closet, as softly lit as the rest of the room. Except for a bust and pedestal in the back, it was empty.

She stepped toward the opening and then paused, thoughts of death-traps and poison darts whirling through her mind. What if she walked in and triggered some kind of a catastrophe? What if the door closed and she was trapped there, and Chris didn't come back?

What if you were the only member of the S.T.A.R.S. who didn't accomplish jack-shit on this entire mission? Show some backbone.

Rebecca steeled herself against the consequences and stepped inside, looking around cautiously. If there was a threat here, she didn't see it. The plain stucco walls were the color of coffee with cream, offset by dark wood trim. The light in the small chamber was provided by a window into a tiny greenhouse on her right, a handful of dying plants behind the dirty glass.

She moved closer to the pedestal at the back, noting that the stone bust on top was of Beethoven; she recognized the stern countenance and heavy brow of the *Moonlight Sonata*'s composer. The pedestal itself boasted a thick gold emblem shaped like a shield or coat of arms, about the size of a dinner plate.

Rebecca crouched down next to the simple pillar, gazing at the emblem. It looked solid and thick, with a vaguely royal design in a paler gold set across the top. It looked familiar; she'd seen the same design somewhere else in the house. . . .

In the dining room, over the fireplace!

Yes, that was it—only the piece over the mantle was made out of wood, she was sure of it. She'd noticed it while Chris was looking at the broken statue.

Curious, she touched the emblem, tracing the pattern across the front—and then grasped the slightly raised edges with both hands and lifted. The heavy emblem came away easily, almost as if it didn't belong there—

—and behind her the secret door rumbled down, sealing her inside.

Without hesitating, she turned and placed the emblem back in its hollow—and the section of wall rose again, sliding up smoothly on hidden tracks. Relieved, she stared down at the heavy gold emblem, thinking.

Someone had rigged all this up in order to keep the medal hidden, so it had to be important—but how was she supposed to remove it? Did the one over the fireplace also reveal a secret passage?

Or . . . is the one over the fireplace the same size?

She couldn't be positive, but she thought it was—and she knew instinctively that it was the right answer. If she switched the two of them, using the wood emblem to keep the door open and placing the gold one over the mantle . . .

Rebecca headed back into the room, smiling. Chris told her to stay put, but she wouldn't be gone more than a minute or two—and perhaps when he got back, she'd have something to show him, a real contribution toward solving the secrets of the mansion.

And proof that she wasn't so useless after all.

ELEVEΠ

BARRY AND JILL STOOD IN THE COVERED walkway by the puzzle lock, breathing the clean night air. Beyond the high walls, the crickets and cicadas hummed their ceaseless song, a soothing reminder that there was still a sane world outside.

Jill's brush with disaster had left her light-headed and somewhat nauseous, and Barry had gently led her to the back door, suggesting that the fresh air would do her good. He hadn't found Chris or Wesker, though he seemed certain that they were still alive. He brought her up to speed quickly, retracing his meandering path through the house as Jill leaned against the wall, still taking deep breaths of the warm air.

". . . and when I heard the shots, I came running." Barry rubbed absently at his short beard. He smiled at her, a somewhat hesitant grin. "Lucky for you.

Another couple of seconds, you would've been a Jill sandwich."

Jill smiled back gratefully, nodding, but noticed that he seemed a little . . . *strained,* the humor forced. Odd. She wouldn't have figured Barry as the type to tense up in the face of danger.

Is it any wonder? We're trapped here, we can't find the team, and this entire mansion is out to get us. Not exactly a laugh-riot.

"I hope I can return the favor if you ever get in a tight spot," she said softly. "Really. You saved my life."

Barry looked away, flushing slightly. "Glad I could help," he said gruffly. "Just be more careful. This place is dangerous."

She nodded again, thinking of how close she'd come to dying. She shivered slightly, then forced the thoughts away; they needed to be concentrating on Chris and Wesker. "So you *do* think they're still alive?"

"Yeah. Besides the shell casings, there was a whole trail of those ghouls in the other wing, all with clean head shots; gotta be Chris—though I had to splatter a couple more of 'em upstairs, so I figure he holed up somewhere along the way. . . ."

Barry nodded toward the copper diagram set into the wall. "So, was this star crest here already?"

Jill frowned, a little surprised at the abrupt change of topic; Chris was one of Barry's closest friends. "No. I found it in another room with a trap. This place seems to be full of them. In fact, maybe we should look for Wesker and Chris together—no telling what they might've stumbled into, or what else could happen to either of us."

Barry shook his head. "I don't know. I mean, you're right, we should watch our step—but there are a lot of rooms, and our first priority ought to be securing an escape. If we split up, we can try to find the rest of these crests, *and* look for Chris at the same time. And Wesker."

Though his demeanor didn't change, Jill had the sudden distinct impression that Barry was uncomfortable. He had turned away to study the copper diagram, but it almost seemed as if he was trying to avoid eye contact.

"Besides," he said, "we know what we're up against now. As long as we use a little common sense, we'll be fine."

"Barry, are you okay? You seem—tired." It wasn't the right word, but it was the only one that came to mind.

He sighed, finally looking at her. He *did* seem tired; there were dark circles under his eyes, and his wide shoulders were slumped.

"No, I'm alright. Just worried about Chris, you know?"

Jill nodded, but she couldn't shake the feeling that there was more to it than that. Since he'd pulled her out of the trap he'd been acting unusually subdued, even nervous.

Paranoid much? This is Barry Burton you're talking about, the backbone of the Raccoon S.T.A.R.S.—not to mention, the man who just saved your life. What could he possibly be hiding?

Jill knew she was probably being overly suspicious—but all the same, she decided to keep her mouth shut about Trent's computer. After all she'd been through, she wasn't feeling particularly trusting. And it sounded like he already had a pretty good idea of the mansion's layout, so it wasn't like he *needed* the information. . . .

That's it, keep rationalizing. Next thing, you'll be suspecting Captain Wesker of planning this whole thing.

Jill scoffed inwardly as she pushed herself away from the wall and she and Barry walked slowly back toward the house. Now *that* was paranoid.

They stopped as they reached the door, Jill taking a few final lungfuls of the sweet air, letting it settle her nerves. Barry had taken out his Colt Python and was reloading the empty chambers, his expression grim.

"I thought I'd go back over to the east wing, see if I can pick up Chris's trail," he said. "Why don't you head upstairs and start looking for the other crests? That way we can cover all of the rooms, work our way back to the main hall. . . ."

Jill nodded and Barry opened the door, the rusty hinges squealing in protest. A wave of cold swept past them and Jill sighed, trying to prepare herself to face another maze of frigid, shadowy halls, another series of unopened doors and the secrets that lay behind them.

"You're gonna do fine," Barry said smoothly, placing a warm hand on her shoulder and gently ushering her back inside. As soon as the door closed behind them he lifted his hand in a casual salute, smiling.

"Good luck," he said, and before she could respond, he turned and hurried away, weapon in hand. With another creak of ancient metal, he slipped through the double doors at the end of the hall and was gone.

Jill stared after him, alone once again in the chilled, stinking silence of the dim corridor. It wasn't her imagination; Barry was keeping something from her. But was it something she needed to worry about, or was he just trying to protect her?

Maybe he found Chris or Wesker, dead, and didn't want to tell me. . . .

It wasn't a pleasant thought, but it would explain his strange, hurried behavior. He obviously wanted them to get out of the house as soon as possible, and wanted her to stay on the west side. And the way he'd fixated on the puzzle mechanism, seeming more concerned with their exit than with Chris's or Wesker's whereabouts. . . .

She looked down at the two crumpled figures in the hall, at the tacky, drying pools of red that surrounded them. Maybe she was trying too hard to find a motive that didn't exist. Maybe, like her, Barry was scared, and sick of feeling like death could come at any time.

Maybe I should stop thinking about it and do my job. Whether or not we find the others, he's right about needing to get out. We have to get back to the city, let people know what's out here. . . .

Jill straightened her shoulders and walked to the door that led to the stairwell, drawing her weapon. She'd made it this far, she could make it a little farther, try to unravel the mystery that had taken the lives of so many—

—or die trying, her mind whispered softly.

Forest Speyer was dead. The laughing, Southern good ol' boy with his ratty clothes and easy grin was no more. That Forest was gone, leaving behind a bloody, lifeless impostor slumped against a wall.

Chris stared down at the impostor, the distant sounds of the night lost to a sudden gust of wind that whipped around the eaves, moaning through the railing of the second-story patio. It was a ghostly sound, but Forest couldn't hear it; Forest would never hear anything again.

Chris crouched down next to the still body, carefully prying Forest's Beretta from beneath cool fingers. He told himself he wouldn't look, but as he reached for Forest's belt pack, he found his gaze fixed on the terrible emptiness where the Bravo's eyes had once been.

Jesus, what happened? What happened to you, man?

Forest's body was covered with wounds, most an inch or two across and surrounded by raw, bloody flesh—it was as if he'd been stabbed hundreds of times with a dull knife, each vicious cut ripping away chunks of skin and muscle. Part of his ribcage was cruelly exposed, slivers of white showing beneath tattered redness. His eyeless, streaming stare was the crowning horror—like the killer hadn't been content to take Forest's life, wanting his soul instead. . . .

There were three clips for the Beretta in Forest's pack. Chris shoved the magazines into a pocket and quickly stood up, tearing his gaze from the mutilated body. He looked out over the dark woods, breathing deeply. His thoughts were jumbled and grasping, trying to find an explanation and yet unable to hold on to any coherent facts.

Once in the main hall, he'd decided to check all of the doors to see which were unlocked—and when he'd seen the bloody hand print in the tiny upstairs hall and heard the wailing cries of birds, he'd charged in, ready to deal out some justice. . . .

. . . *crows. It sounded like crows, an entire flock . . . or a murder, actually. Pack of dogs, kindle of kittens, murder of crows . . .*

He blinked, his tired mind focusing on the seemingly random bit of trivia. Frowning, Chris crouched back down next to Forest's ravaged body, studying the jagged wounds closely. There were dozens of tiny scratches amidst the more serious cuts, scratches set into lined patterns—

Claws. Talons.

Even as the thought occurred to him, he heard a restless flutter of wings. He turned slowly, still holding Forest's Beretta in a hand that had suddenly gone cold.

A sleek, monstrous bird was perched on the railing not two feet away, watching him with bright black eyes. Its smooth feathers gleamed dully against its bloated body . . . and a ribbon of something red and wet hung from its beak.

The bird tilted its head to the side and let out a tremendous shriek, the streamer of Forest's flesh dropping to the railing. From all around, the answering cries of its gathered siblings flooded the night air. There was a furious whisper of oversized wings as dozens of dark, fluttering shapes swooped out from beneath the eaves, screeching and clawing.

Chris ran, the image of Forest's bloody, terrible eyes burned into his pounding thoughts as he lunged for escape. He stumbled into the tiny hall and slammed the door against the rising screams of the birds, adrenaline pumping through his system in hot, surging beats.

He took a deep breath, then another, and after a moment, his heart slowed down to a more normal pace. The shrieks of the crows gradually grew distant, blown away on a softly moaning wind.

Jesus, how dumb can I get? Stupid, stupid—

He'd stormed out onto the deck looking for a fight, looking to avenge the deaths of the other S.T.A.R.S.—and been shocked into stupidity by what he'd found. If he hadn't let himself get so freaked out by Forest's death, he would have made the connection sooner between the birds and the types of wounds—and perhaps noticed the gathering flesh-eaters that had watched him from the shadows, looking for their next victim.

He headed for the door back to the main hall, angry with himself for going into a situation unprepared. He couldn't afford to keep making mistakes, to let his attention wander from what was in front of him. This wasn't some kind of a game, where he could push a reset button if he missed a trick. People were dying, his *friends* were dying—

—and if you don't pull your head out of your ass and

*start being more careful, you're going to join them—
another torn and lifeless body crumpled in a cold
hallway somewhere, another victim to the insanity of
this house—*

Chris silenced the nagging whisper, taking a deep
breath as he stepped back into the high gallery of the
lobby and closed the door behind him. Beating himself up was no more useful than charging blindly
around in a strange and dangerous environment,
looking for revenge. He had to concentrate on what
was important: the lost Alphas and Rebecca. . . .

He walked toward the stairs, tucking Forest's weapon into his waistband. At least Rebecca would be able
to defend herself—

"Chris."

Startled, he looked down to see the young
S.T.A.R.S. member at the base of the wide steps,
grinning up at him.

He jogged down the stairs, glad to see her in spite of
himself. "What happened? Is everything all right?"

Rebecca held up a silver key as he reached her, still
smiling widely. "I found something I thought you
could use."

He took the key, noting that the handle was etched
with a tiny shield before slipping it inside his vest.
Rebecca was beaming, her eyes flashing with excitement.

"After you left, I played the piano and this secret
door opened up in the wall. There was this gold
emblem inside, like a shield, and I switched it with
the one in the dining room—and the grandfather
clock moved, and that key was behind it—"

She broke off suddenly, her smile faltering as she studied his face. "I'm sorry . . . I know I shouldn't have left, but I thought I could catch you before you got too far . . ."

"It's okay," he said, forcing a smile. "I'm just surprised to see you. Here, I found you something a little better than a can of insect repellent."

He handed her the Beretta, pulling out a couple of clips to go with it. Rebecca took the gun, staring down at it thoughtfully.

When she looked up at him again, her gaze was serious and intense. "Who was it?"

Chris thought about lying, but saw that she wasn't going to buy it—and realized suddenly what it was about her that made him feel so protective, that made him want to shield her from the sad and sickening truth.

Claire.

That was it; Rebecca reminded him of his little sister, from her tomboy sarcasm and quick wit to the way she wore her hair.

"Listen," she said quietly, "I know you feel responsible for me, and I admit that I'm pretty new at this. But I'm a member of this team, and sheltering me from the facts could get me killed. So—who was it?"

Chris stared at her for a moment and then sighed. She was right. "Forest. I found him outside, he'd been pecked to death by crows. Kenneth's dead, too."

A sudden anguish passed across her eyes, but she nodded firmly, keeping her gaze on his. "Okay. So what do we do now?"

Chris couldn't help the slightest of smiles, trying to remember if he'd ever been so young.

He motioned up the stairs, hoping that he wasn't about to make another mistake. "I guess we try another door. . . ."

Wesker didn't catch much of the conversation between Barry and Jill, but after a muffled, "Good luck," from Mr. Burton, he heard a door open and close somewhere near by—and a moment later, the hollow thump of bootsteps against wood, followed by another closing door. The hall outside was clear, his team off on their mission to find the rest of the copper crests.

Looks like I picked the right room to wait in. . . .

He'd used the helmet key to lock himself into a small study by the back door, the perfect place from which to monitor the team's progress. Not only could he hear them coming and going, he'd be able to get a head start to the labs. . . .

He held the heavy wind crest up to the light of the desk lamp, grinning. It had been too easy, really. He'd happened across the plaster statue on his way back from talking to Barry, and remembered that it had a secret compartment somewhere. Rather than waste valuable time searching, he'd simply pushed the hideous thing off the dining room balcony. It hadn't been hiding one of the crests, but the sparkle of the blue jewel amidst the rubble had been almost as good. There was a room just off the dining hall that held a statue of a tiger with one red eye and one blue, one of the few mechanisms that he'd remembered from an earlier visit. A quick visit to the statue had confirmed his suspicions; both eyes had been missing, and when he'd placed the gaudy blue jewel into its proper socket, the tiger had turned to one side and presented him with the crest. Just like that, he was one step closer to completing his mission.

When the other three are in place, I'll wait until they're off looking for the final piece and then slip right out the door. . . .

He considered going to check the diagram, but decided against it. The house was big, but not *that* big, and there was no need to expose himself to further risk of being seen. Besides, they probably hadn't managed to find any of the other crests yet. He'd already had a close call when he'd gone downstairs to retrieve the jewel, almost stepping directly into Chris Redfield's path. Chris had found the rookie and the two of them were blundering around, probably looking for "clues." . . .

Besides, this room is comfortable. Maybe I'll take a nap while I wait for the rest of them to catch up.

He leaned back in the desk chair, pleased with himself for all he'd accomplished so far. What could have been a disaster was turning out quite nicely, thanks to some quick thinking on his part. He had already found one of the crests, he had Barry and Jill working for him—and he'd had the good fortune to run into Ellen Smith while he'd been in the library. . . .

Oops, scratch that. It's Doctor *Ellen Smith, thank you very much.*

After fetching the wind crest, he'd gone to the

library to check the small side room that overlooked the estate's heliport, the entrance concealed behind a bookcase. A quick search had revealed nothing useful, and he'd been about to check the back room when Dr. Smith had shambled out to greet him.

He had tried to get a date with her ever since he'd moved to Raccoon, drawn in by her long legs and platinum blond hair; he'd always been partial to blonds, particularly smart ones. Not only had she repeatedly turned him down, she hadn't even tried to be nice about it. When he'd called her Ellen, she'd coolly informed him that she was his superior *and* a doctor, and would be addressed as such. Ice queen, through and through. If she hadn't been so damned good-looking, he never would've bothered in the first place.

But my, how your beauty has faded, Dr. Ellen. . . .

Wesker closed his eyes, smiling, reliving the experience. It had been the ratty strings of blond hair that had given her away as she'd shuffled out from behind a shelf, moaning and reaching for him. Her legs were still long, but they'd lost a lot of their appeal—not to mention a fair amount of skin. . . .

"What lovely perfume you're wearing, Dr. Smith," he'd said. Then two shots to the head, and she'd gone down in a spray of blood and bone. Wesker didn't like to think of himself as a shallow man, but pulling the trigger on that high-riding bitch had been wonderfully—no, deeply—gratifying.

Like icing on a cake, a little bonus perk for taking matters in hand. Maybe if I'm lucky I'll run into that prick Sarton down in the labs. . . .

After a few moments, Wesker stood up and stretched, turning to scan some of the titles on the bookshelf behind him. He was eager to get moving, but it might take the S.T.A.R.S. awhile to find the rest of the puzzle pieces and there was really nothing he could do to hurry the process; he might as well keep busy. . . .

He frowned, struggling to make sense of the technical titles. One of the books was called, *Phagemids: Alpha Complementation Vectors,* the next one was, *cDNA Libraries and Electrophoresis Conditions.*

Biochemistry texts and medical journals, terrific. Maybe he'd get that nap in after all. Just reading the titles was making him sleepy.

His gaze fell across a heavy-looking tome sitting by itself on one of the lower shelves, bound in a fine red leather. He picked it up, glad to see a title he could read printed across the front, even one as stupid as, *Eagle of East, Wolf of West.* . . .

Wait—that's the same thing written on the fountain—

Wesker stared at the words, feeling his good mood slipping away. It couldn't be, the researchers had gone nuts but surely they wouldn't have locked down the labs, there was no reason for it. He opened the book almost frantically, praying that he was wrong—

—and let out a low moan of helpless rage at what was tucked into the sham book's glued pages. A brass medallion with an eagle engraved on it lay in the cut away compartment—part of a key to yet another of Spencer's insane locks.

It was like the punch line to a cruel joke. To get out

of the house, he had to find the crests. Once out in the courtyard, he'd have to make his way through a winding maze of tunnels that ended in a hidden section of the garden—where there was an old stone fountain that marked the entrance to the underground labs. The fountain was one of Spencer's fanciful creations, a marvel of engineering that could be opened and closed to hide the facility underneath—provided, of course, that you had the keys: two medallions made out of brass, an eagle on one, a wolf on the other. . . .

Finding the eagle meant that the gate was closed. And *that* meant that the wolf could be anywhere, anywhere at all—and that his chances of even getting to the lab had just dropped down to somewhere near zero.

Unable to control his fury, he snatched up the medal and threw the book against the desk, knocking the lamp over with a crash and plunging the room into sudden blackness. There was no longer any point in holding on to the wind crest; his perfect plan was ruined. He'd have to give up his edge and hope that one of the others would inadvertently stumble across the wolf medal for him, secreted away somewhere on the massive, sprawling estate.

Which means more risk, more searching—and a chance that one of them will reach the labs before I do.

Seething, Wesker stood in the dark silence with his fists clenched, trying not to scream.

†WELVE

JILL HEARD SOMETHING LIKE BREAKING glass and held perfectly still, listening. The acoustics of the mansion were strange, the long corridors and unusual floor plan making it hard to tell where sounds were coming from.

Or if you even heard them at all. . . .

She sighed, taking a last look around the quiet, book-lined sitting room at the top of the stairs. She'd already checked the three other rooms along the gallery railing and found exactly nothing of interest— a sparse bedroom with two bunks, an office, and an unfinished den with a locked door and a fireplace inside. The only switches she'd found were light switches, though she *had* gotten excited over a rather sinister-looking black button on the wall of the office—until she'd pushed it, and found that she'd managed to discover the drainage control for an empty fish tank in the corner.

She'd found some ammo for the Remington, she supposed she should be grateful for that—a dozen shells in a metal box underneath one of the bunks in the bedroom. But if there'd been any hidden crests, she'd missed them.

Jill took out Trent's computer and checked the map, finding her position at the top of the stairs. Just past the sitting room's second door was a wide, U-shaped corridor that angled back around to the front hall balcony. The corridor also connected to two rooms, one a dead end and the other leading through several more. . . .

She put the computer away and drew her Beretta, taking a moment to clear her mind before stepping into the corridor. It wasn't easy. Between trying to figure out what had happened in the house to create monsters and her concerns for and about her team, her thoughts were distinctly messy.

Should've looked closer at those papers. . . .

The office had been simple, a desk, a bookshelf— but there was a rack of lab coats by the door and the papers strewn across the desk had mostly been lists of numbers and letters. She knew just enough chemistry to know that she was *looking* at chemistry, so she didn't bother trying to read them—but since finding the papers, she had begun to think of the zombies as the result of a research accident. The mansion was too well maintained to have come from private money, and the fact that it had been kept a secret for so long suggested a cover up. She guessed that there was a couple of months worth of dust on almost everything—which coincided with the first attacks in Raccoon. If the people in the house had been conducting some kind of an experiment and something had gone wrong . . .

Something that transformed them into flesh-eating ghouls? That's a bit far-fetched. . . .

But it made more sense than anything else she could come up with, although she'd keep her mind open to other possibilities. As to her concerns about the team—Barry was acting weird and Chris and Wesker were still missing; no new developments there.

And there won't be any if you don't get going.

Right. Jill put her musings on hold and stepped out into the hall.

She noticed the smell before she actually saw the zombie farther down the corridor, crumpled to the floor. The small wall sconces cast an uneven glow over the body, reflecting off of dark red trim and tinting everything in the corridor a smoky crimson. She trained her weapon on the still body—and heard a door closing somewhere close by.

Barry?

He'd said he was going to be in the mansion's other wing, but maybe he'd found something and had come looking for her . . . or maybe she was finally going to meet up with someone else from the team.

Smiling at the thought she hurried down the gloomy hall, eager to see another familiar face. As she neared the corner, a fresh wave of decay washed over her—

—and the fallen creature at her feet grabbed at her boot, clutching her ankle with surprising strength.

Startled, Jill flailed her arms to keep her balance, crying out in disgust as the slobbering zombie inched its rotting face toward her boot. Its peeling, skeletal fingers scrabbled weakly at the thick leather, seeking a firmer grip—

—and Jill instinctively brought her other boot down on the back of its head, the heavy treads sliding across the skull with a sickening wet sound. A wide piece of flaking scalp tore away, revealing glistening bone. The creature kept clawing at her, oblivious to pain.

The second and third kicks hit the back of its neck—and on the fourth, she felt as much as heard the dull *snap* of vertebrae giving out, crushed beneath her heel.

The pale hands fluttered and with a choking, liquid sigh, the zombie settled to the musty carpet.

Jill stepped over the limp body and ran around the corner, swallowing back bile. She was convinced that the pitiful creatures roaming the halls were victims somehow, just as much as Becky and Pris had been, and releasing them to death was a kindness—but they were also a menace, not to mention morbidly unwholesome. She had to be more cautious.

There was a door to her right, heavy wood overlaid with twining metal designs. There was a picture of armor over the key plate, but like the other doors she'd come across upstairs, it was unlocked.

There was no one inside the well-lit room but she hesitated, suddenly reluctant to continue her search for whoever else was wandering the area. Two walls of the large chamber were lined with full suits of armor, eight to a side, and there was a small display case at the back—not to mention a large red switch set into the middle of the gray tiled floor.

Another trap? Or a puzzle. . . .

Intrigued, she walked into the room and headed for the glass fronted display, the silent, lifeless guards seeming to watch her every move. There were a couple of mysterious grated holes in the floor, one on either side of the red switch, for ventilation perhaps—and she felt her heart speed up a little, suddenly sure that she had found another of the mansion's traps.

A quick inspection of the dusty display case decided it for her; there wasn't any way that she could see to open it, the glass front a single thick piece. And something in one shadowy niche at the bottom glinted like dull copper. . . .

I'm supposed to push that button, thinking that it will open the case—and then what?

She had a sudden vivid image of the ventilation holes sealing off and the door locking itself, a death by slow suffocation in an airless tomb. The chamber could fill with water, or some kind of poisonous gas. She looked around the room, frowning, wondering if she should try to block the door open or if perhaps there was another switch hidden in one of the empty suits. . . .

. . . every riddle has more than one answer, Jilly, don't forget it.

Jill grinned suddenly. Why push the button at all?

She crouched down next to the case and took a firm grip on the barrel of her handgun. With a single firm *tap,* the glass cracked, thin lines spidering away from the impact. She used the butt of the gun to knock out a thick chunk and reached carefully inside.

She withdrew a hexagonal copper crest, engraved with an archaic smiling sun. She smiled back at it, pleased with her solution. Apparently some of the house's tricks could be worked around, provided she ignored a few rules of fair play. All the same, she found herself hurrying back to the door, not wanting to call it a win until she was clear of the solemn chamber.

Stepping back into the blood-hued corridor, she stood for a moment, holding the crest as she weighed her options. She could continue to look for whoever had closed that door, or head back to the puzzle lock and place the crest. As much as she wanted to find her team, Barry had been right about needing to get out of the mansion. If any of the other S.T.A.R.S. were still alive, they'd surely also be looking for an escape. . . .

Her thoughtful gaze fell across the fetid, broken creature that she'd killed, lingering on the slowly spreading pool of dark fluids surrounding its scabby head—and she realized suddenly that she desperately wanted to leave the house, to escape its tainted air and the pestilent creatures that stalked its cold and dusty halls. She wanted *out,* and as soon as was humanly possible.

Her decision made, Jill hurried back the way she'd come, gripping the heavy crest tightly. She'd already uncovered two of the pieces that the S.T.A.R.S needed to escape the mansion. She didn't know what they'd be escaping *to*, but anything had to be better than what they would leave behind. . . .

"Richard!" Rebecca immediately dropped to her knees next to the Bravo, feeling his throat for a pulse with one trembling hand.

Chris stared mutely down at the torn body, already knowing that she wouldn't find a heartbeat; the gaping wound on Richard Aiken's right shoulder was drying, no fresh blood seeping through the mutilated tissue. He was dead.

He watched Rebecca's slender hand slowly drop away from the Bravo's neck and then reach up to close his glazed, unseeing eyes. Her shoulders slumped. Chris felt sick over their discovery; the communications expert had been a positive, sweet guy, and only twenty-three years old. . . .

He looked around the silent room, searching randomly for some clue as to how Richard had died. The room they'd entered just off the second-floor balcony was undecorated and empty. Except for Richard, there was nothing—

Frowning, Chris took a few steps toward the room's second entrance and crouched down, brushing at the dark tile floor. There was a dried crust of blood in the shape of a boot heel between Richard's body and the plain wooden door ten feet away. He stared at the door thoughtfully, tightening his hold on the Beretta.

Whatever killed him is on the other side, maybe waiting for more victims—

"Chris, take a look at this."

Rebecca was still kneeling by Richard, her gaze fixed on the bloody mass of his torn shoulder. Chris joined her, not sure what he was supposed to be looking at. The wound was ragged and messy, the flesh discolored by trauma. Strange, though, how it didn't seem very deep. . . .

"See those purple lines, radiating out from the cuts? And the way the muscle has been punctured, here and here?" She pointed out two dark holes about six inches apart, each surrounded by skin that had turned an infected-looking red.

Rebecca sat back on her heels, looking up at him. "I think he was poisoned. It looks like a snake bite."

Chris stared at her. "What snake gets that big?"

She shook her head, standing. "Got me. Maybe it was something else. But that wound shouldn't have killed him, it would have taken hours for him to bleed out. I'm pretty sure he was poisoned."

Chris regarded her with new respect; she had a good eye for details and was handling herself remarkably well, considering.

He searched Richard's body quickly, coming up with another full clip and a short-wave radio. He handed both to Rebecca, tucking Richard's empty Beretta into his waistband.

He looked at the door again, then back at Rebecca. "Whatever killed him might be back there. . . ."

"Then we'll have to be careful," she said. Without another word, she walked to the door and stood there, waiting for him.

I've gotta stop thinking of her as a kid. She's outlived

most of the rest of her team already, she doesn't need me to patronize her or tell her to wait behind.

He stepped up to the door and nodded at her. She turned the knob and pushed it open, both of them raising their weapons as they edged into a narrow hallway.

Straight ahead were a few wood steps leading to a closed door. To their left, an offshoot of the hall, another door at the end. There was blood smeared on the walls bordering the steps, and Chris was suddenly certain that it was Richard's; his killer was behind that door.

He motioned down the offshoot, speaking quietly. "You take that room. You run into any trouble, come back here and wait. Check back in five minutes either way."

Rebecca nodded and moved down the narrow hall. Chris waited until she'd gone into the room before climbing the steps, his heart already thudding solidly against his ribs.

The door was locked, but Chris saw that there was a tiny shield etched next to keyhole. Rebecca was turning out to be more useful than he could have possibly imagined. He took out the key she'd given him and unlocked the wide door, checking his Beretta before moving inside.

It was a large attic, as plain and unassuming as the rest of the mansion was ornate. Wooden support beams extended from the floor to the sloping ceiling, and other than a few boxes and barrels against the walls, it was empty.

Chris walked farther in, his guard up as he scanned for movement. At the other side of the long room was a partial wall, maybe four feet by nine, standing several feet from the back of the attic. It reminded him of a horse stall, and it was the only area that wasn't open to view. Chris moved toward it slowly, his boots against the wood floor sending hollow echoes through the cool air.

He edged to the wall, training his Beretta over the top as he peered down, heart pounding.

No snake, but there was a jagged hole near the floorboards between the two walls, a foot high and a couple across—and a strange, acrid odor, musky, like the smell of some wild animal. Frowning at the scent, Chris started to back away—

—and stopped, leaning in closer. There was a rounded piece of metal next to the hole, like a penny the size of a small fist. There was something engraved on it, a crescent shape. . . .

Chris walked around the side and into the stall, keeping a wary eye on the hole as he crouched down and picked up the metal piece. It was a six-sided disk of copper with a moon on it, a nice bit of craftsmanship—

Inside the hole, a soft, sliding sound.

Chris jumped back, targeting the opening as he moved. He backed up quickly until his shoulders brushed the attic wall, then started to edge away—

—and a dark cylinder shot out of the opening, lightning fast. It was as big around as a dinner plate and it hit the wall inches from his right leg, wood crunching from the impact—

—oh shit that's a SNAKE—

Chris stumbled away as the giant reptile reared back, pulling more of its long, dusky body out of the wall. Hissing, it raised up, lifting its head as high as Chris's chest and exposing dripping fangs.

Chris ran halfway across the room and spun, firing at the massive, diamond-shaped head. The snake let out a strange, hissing cry as a shot tore through one side of its gaping mouth, punching a hole through the tightly stretched skin.

It dropped back to the floor and whipped itself toward him with a single waving push of its muscular body, at least twenty feet long. Chris fired again and a chunk of scaly flesh erupted from the snake's back, dark blood spewing from the wound.

With another roaring hiss, the animal reared up in front of him, its head only inches away from Chris's gun, blood gushing from the hole in its mouth—

—Eyes. Get the eyes—

Chris pulled the trigger and the snake fell across him, knocking him to the floor, its body thrashing wildly. The tail slammed into one of the thick support beams hard enough to crack it as Chris struggled to free his pinned arms, to at least hurt it worse before he died—

—and the cold, heavy body suddenly went limp, sagging bonelessly to the floor.

"Chris!" Rebecca rushed into the room, and stopped cold, staring at the monstrous reptile. "Woah. . . ."

His boot found one of the wooden supports and with a tremendous shove, Chris managed to wiggle out from beneath the thick body. Rebecca reached down to help him up, her eyes wide with awe.

They stared down at the wound that had killed the creature—the black, liquid hole where its right eye had been, obliterated by a nine-millimeter slug.

"Are you okay?" She asked softly.

Chris nodded; a few bruised ribs maybe, but so what? He'd literally been inches from certain death, and all because he'd stopped to—

He held up the copper crest, having to pry his clenched fingers from around the thick metal. He'd held onto it throughout the attack without even realizing it—and looking at it now, he had a gut feeling that it was important somehow. . . .

. . . maybe because you were almost snake-food for picking it up?

Rebecca took it from him, tracing a finger over the engraved moon.

"You find anything?" he asked.

Rebecca shook her head. "Table, couple of shelves . . . what's this for, anyway?"

Chris shrugged, looking back down at the bloody hole where the snake's shining eye had been. He shuddered involuntarily, thinking of what would have happened if he'd missed that final shot. . . .

"Maybe we'll figure it out somewhere along the way," he said quietly. "Come on, let's get out of here."

Rebecca handed the crest back to him and together they hurried out of the cold attic. As he closed the door behind them, Chris realized suddenly that although he'd never cared before, he now absolutely hated snakes.

Barry walked heavily up the stairs in the main hall, the knot of dread in the pit of his stomach tightening with each step. He'd been through every room he could open in the east wing and had come up empty-handed.

The same horrible images played through his mind over and over as he trudged up the steps. Kathy and Moira and Poly Anne, terrified and suffering at the hands of strangers in their own home. Kathy knew the combination to the gun safe in the basement, but the chances of her making it down the stairs before someone could get in—

Barry reached the first landing and took a deep, shaky breath. Kathy wouldn't even think to run for the weapons if she heard someone breaking through one of the windows or doors. Her first priority would be to get to the girls, to make sure they were okay.

If I don't turn up those crests soon, nothing will be okay.

He hadn't seen a phone or radio anywhere in the house. If Wesker couldn't get to that laboratory, how would he be able to contact the people at White Umbrella and call off the killers?

Barry reached the door on the upper landing that led into the west wing. His only hope was that either Jill or Wesker had managed to find the three missing pieces. He didn't know where Wesker was (although he had no doubts that the rat-bastard would turn up soon enough), but Jill would probably still be searching upstairs. They could split up the rooms she hadn't checked and at least rule out the least likely areas. If they couldn't uncover any more of the crests, he'd have to go back through the east wing and start ripping apart furniture. . . .

He opened the door that led into the red hallway, lost in thought—and very nearly ran into Chris Redfield and Rebecca Chambers as they stepped out of the doorway on his right.

Chris's face lit up with a broad, beaming grin. "Barry!"

The younger man stepped forward and embraced him roughly, then backed up, still grinning. "Jesus, it's good to see you! I was starting to think that me and Rebecca were the last ones alive—where are Jill and Wesker?"

Barry pasted a smile on as he fumbled for an acceptable answer, feeling almost sick with guilt. Lying to Jill hadn't been easy, but he'd known Chris for *years*—

—Kathy and the girls, dead—

"Jill and I came after you, but all the doors in that hall were locked—and when we got back to the lobby, the captain was gone. Since then, we've been looking for you two and trying to find a way out. . . ."

Barry smiled more naturally. "It's good to see you, too. Both of you."

At least that much is true.

"So Wesker just disappeared?" Chris asked.

Barry nodded, uncomfortable. "Yeah. And we found Ken. One of those ghouls got to him."

Chris sighed. "I saw. Forest and Richard are dead, too."

Barry felt a wave of sadness and swallowed thickly, suddenly hating Wesker even more. The people Wesker worked for had done this and now they wanted to cover it all up, avoiding responsibility for their actions—

—and like it or not, I'm going to help them do it.

Barry took a deep breath and fixed an image of his wife and daughters in his mind's eye. "Jill found a back door, and we think it could be a way out—except its got this trick lock, like a puzzle, and we have to get all the pieces together to open it. There are these four metal crests, made out of copper—Jill got one already, and we think the rest are hidden throughout the mansion. . . ."

He trailed off at Chris's sudden grin as Chris reached into his vest. "Something like this?"

Barry stared at the crest that Chris had produced, feeling his heart speed up. "Yeah, that's one of them! Where'd you find it?"

Rebecca spoke up, smiling shyly. "He had to fight a big snake for it—a *really* big snake. I think it may have been affected by the accident, though a cross-genus virus . . . those are pretty rare."

Barry reached for the crest as casually as he could manage, frowning. "Accident?"

Chris nodded. "We found some information that suggests there's some kind of secret research facility here on the estate—and that something they were working on got loose. A virus."

"One that can apparently infect mammals and

reptiles," Rebecca added. "Not just different species, different *families.*"

It's certainly infected mine, Barry thought bleakly.

He let his frown deepen, feigning thoughtfulness as he struggled to come up with an excuse to get away. The captain wouldn't approach him unless he was alone, and he was desperate to get the copper piece into place, to prove that he was still on board, cooperating—and that he'd convinced the rest of the team to help him look. He could feel the seconds ticking away, the metal growing warm beneath his sweating fingers.

"We need to get the feds in on this," he said finally, "a full investigation, military support, quarantine of the area—"

Chris and Rebecca were both nodding, and again Barry felt nearly overwhelmed by guilt. God, if only they weren't so *trusting—*

"—but to do that, we have to find all of these crests. Jill might've turned up another one by now, maybe both of them. . . ."

. . . I can only pray . . .

"Do you know where she is?" Chris asked.

Barry nodded, thinking fast. "I'm pretty sure, but this place is kind of a maze . . . why don't you wait in the main hall while I go get her? That way we can organize our search, do a more thorough job—"

He smiled, hoping it looked more convincing than it felt. "—though if we don't turn up soon, keep looking for more of those pieces. The back door is at the end of the west wing corridors, first floor."

Chris just stared at him for a moment, and Barry

could see the questions forming in his bright gaze, questions that Barry wouldn't be able to answer: Why split up at all? What about finding the missing captain? How could he be certain that the back door was an escape?

Please, please just do as I say—

"Okay," Chris said reluctantly. "We'll wait, but if she's not where you think she is, come back and get us. We stand a better chance of making it through this place if we stick together."

Barry nodded, and before Chris could say anything more, he turned and jogged away down the dim hall. He'd seen the hesitation in Chris's eyes, heard the uncertainty in his voice—and with his final words, Barry had felt himself wanting desperately to warn his friend of Wesker's betrayal. Leaving was the only way to keep himself from saying something he might regret, something that might get his family killed.

As soon as he heard the door back to the balcony close, he picked up speed, taking the corners at a full run. There was a dead zombie near the door that led to the stairs, and Barry leaped over it, the stench falling away as he ducked through the connecting passage. He took the back stairs three at a time as his conscience yammered mercilessly away at him, reminding him of his treachery.

You're a liar, Barry, using your friends the way Wesker's using you, playing on their trust. You could've told them what was really going on, let them help you put a stop to it—

Barry shook the thoughts away as he reached the door to the covered walk, slamming the heavy metal aside. He couldn't risk it, *wouldn't*—what if Wesker had been nearby, had overheard? The captain had Barry's family to blackmail him with, but once Chris and the others knew the truth, what was to stop Wesker from just killing them? If he helped Wesker destroy the evidence, the S.T.A.R.S. wouldn't be able to prove anything, the captain could just let them all walk away—

Barry reached the diagram next to the back door and stopped, staring. Relief flooded through him, cool and sweet. Three of the four openings were filled, the sun, wind, and star crests in place. It was over.

He can get to the lab now, call off his people, he doesn't need us anymore! I can go back in and keep the team busy while he does whatever he has to do, the RPD will show eventually and we can forget this ever happened—

He was so elated that he didn't register the muted footsteps on the stone path behind him, didn't realize that he wasn't alone anymore until Wesker's smooth voice spoke up beside him.

"Why don't you finish the puzzle, Mr. Burton?"

Barry jumped, startled. He glared at Wesker, loathing the smug, bland face behind the sunglasses. Wesker smiled, nodding his head at the copper crest in Barry's hand.

"Yeah, right," Barry muttered darkly, and slipped the final piece into place. There was a thick metallic sound from inside the door, *ka-chink*—

—and Wesker walked past him, pushing the door open to reveal a small, well-used tool shed. Barry peered inside, saw the exit at the opposite wall. There was no diagram set next to it, no more crazy puzzles to figure out.

Kathy and the girls were safe.

With a low bow, Wesker motioned for Barry to step inside the shed, still smiling.

"Time's short, Barry, and there's still a lot for us to do."

Barry stared at him, confused. "What do you mean? You can get to the lab now . . ."

"Well, there's been a slight change of plans. See, it turns out that I need to find something else, and I have an idea of where it might be, but there are some dangers involved . . . and you've done such a good job so far, I want you to come along—"

Wesker's smile transformed into a shark-like grin, a cold, pitiless reminder of what was at stake.

"—in fact, I'm afraid that I'm going to have to *insist* on it."

After a long, terrible moment, Barry nodded helplessly.

✝ Thirteen

My dearest Alma,

I sit here trying to think of where to begin, of how to explain in a few simple words all that's happened in my life since we last spoke, and already I fail. I hope this letter finds you well and whole, and that you will forgive the tangents of my pen; this isn't easy for me. Even as I write, I can feel the simplest of concepts slipping away, lost to feelings of despair and confusion—but I have to tell you what's in my heart before I can rest. Be patient, and accept that what I tell you is the truth.

The entire story would take hours for me to tell you, and time is short, so accept these things as fact: last month there was an accident in the lab and the virus we were studying escaped. All my colleagues who were infected are dead or dying, and the nature of the disease is such that those still living have lost their senses. This virus robs its victims of their humanity, forcing them in their sickness to seek out and destroy life. Even as I write these words, I can hear them, pressing against my locked door like mindless, hungry animals, crying out like lost souls.

There aren't words true enough, deep enough to describe the sorrow and shame that I feel knowing that I had a hand in their creation. I believe that they feel nothing now, no fear or pain—but that they can't experience the horror of what they've become doesn't free me of my terrible burden. I am, in part, responsible for this nightmare that surrounds me.

In spite of the guilt that is burned into my very being, that will haunt my every breath, I might have tried to survive, if only to see you again. But my best efforts only delayed the inevitable; I am infected, and there is no cure for what will follow—except to end my life before I lose the only thing that separates me from them. My love for you.

Please understand. Please know that I'm sorry.

Martin Crackhorn

Jill sighed, laying the crumpled paper gently on the desk. The creatures *were* victims of their own research. It seemed she'd had the right idea about what had happened in the mansion, though reading the heartfelt letter put a serious damper on any pride she might have taken from her deduction skills. After placing the sun crest, she'd decided that the upstairs office merited a closer look—and with a little digging, she'd found the final scrawled testament of Crackhorn, tucked in a drawer.

Crackhorn, Martin Crackhorn—that was one of the names on Trent's list. . . .

Jill frowned, walking slowly back to the office door. For some reason, Trent wanted the S.T.A.R.S. to figure out what had happened at the mansion before anyone else did—but with as much as he obviously knew about it, why not just tell them outright? And what did he stand to gain by telling them anything at all?

She stepped through the office's small foyer and back out into the hall, still frowning. Barry had been acting strange before, and she needed to find out why. Maybe she could get a straight answer if she just asked him outright. . . .

Or maybe not. Either way, it'll tell me something.

Jill stopped by the back stairs, taking a deep breath—and realized that something was different. She looked around uncertainly, trying to figure out what it was her senses were telling her.

It's warmer. Just a little, but it's definitely warmer. And the air isn't quite as stale. . . .

Like someone had opened a window. Or maybe a door.

Jill turned and jogged down the stairs, suddenly anxious to check the puzzle lock. Reaching the bottom of the steps, she saw that the door connecting one hall to the next was standing open. She could hear crickets singing faintly, feel the fresh night air wafting toward her through the frigid mustiness of the house.

She hurried to the darker corridor and hooked a right, trying not to get her hopes up. Another sharp right and she could see the door that led to the covered walkway standing open.

Maybe that's all it is, it doesn't mean the puzzle's solved. . . .

Jill broke into a run, feeling the clean warmth of summer air against her skin as she rounded the corner in the stone path—

—and let out a short, triumphant laugh as she saw the four placed crests next to the open door. A warm breeze was flowing through the room that the puzzle had unlocked, a small storage shed for gardening tools. The metal door on the wall opposite was standing open, and Jill could see moonlight playing across a brick wall just past the rusted hinges.

Barry had been right, the door led outside. They'd be able to get help now, find a safe route through the woods or at least signal—

But if Barry found the missing pieces, why didn't he come looking for me?

Jill's grin faded as she stepped into the shed, absently taking in the dusty boxes and barrels that lined the gray stone walls. Barry had known where she was, had suggested himself that she take the second floor of the west wing. . . .

So maybe it wasn't Barry who opened the door.

True, it could've been Chris or Wesker or one of the Bravos. If that was the case, she should probably go back in and look for Barry.

Or investigate a little first, make sure it's worth the effort.

It was a bit of a rationalization, but she had to admit to herself that the thought of returning to the mansion with a possible escape in front of her wasn't all that enticing. She unholstered her Beretta and walked toward the outer door, her decision made.

The first thing she noticed was the sound of rushing water over the soft forest noises that filled the cooling air, like a waterfall. The second and third were the bodies of the two dogs that lay across the irregular stone path, shot to death.

Pretty safe bet that one of the S.T.A.R.S. came this way. . . .

Jill edged out into a high-walled courtyard, low hedges set into brick planters on either side. Dark clouds hung oppressively low overhead. Across the open space was a barred iron gate just past an island of shrubs; to her left, a straight path overshadowed by the ten-foot-high brick walls that bordered it. The gentle waterfall sound seemed to come from that direction, though the path ended abruptly in a metal gate a few feet high.

Stairs going down maybe?

Jill hesitated, looked back at the arched, rusty gate in front of her and then at the curled bodies of the mutant dogs. They were both closer to the gate than the walkway, and assuming they'd been killed while attacking, the shooter would have been headed in that direction—

There was a sudden sound of water splashing wildly, making the decision for her. Jill turned and ran down the moonlit walk, hoping to catch a glimpse of whatever was making the noise.

She reached the end of the stone path and leaned over the gate—then drew back a little, surprised by the sudden drop off. There were no stairs, the gate opened to a tiny platform elevator and a huge, open courtyard, twenty feet below.

The splashing was off to the right, and Jill looked down and across the wide yard just in time to see a shadowy figure walk through the waterfall she'd heard, disappearing behind the curtain of water that cascaded down the west wall.

What the hell—

She stared at the small waterfall, blinking, not sure if her eyes were playing tricks on her. The splashing had stopped as soon as the person disappeared, and she was fairly certain that she wasn't hearing things— which meant that the rushing water concealed a secret passage.

Great, that's just what this place needs. Lord knows I didn't get enough of that inside.

The controls for the one-man lift were on a metal bar next to the rusting gate, the platform itself down in the courtyard. Jill toggled the power switch, but nothing happened. She'd have to get down another way, wasting time while the mysterious splasher got farther away.

Unless . . .

Jill looked down the narrow elevator shaft, an inset square only three feet across and open on the side facing the yard. Coming up would be a bitch, but descending? Cake. She could crouch her way down in a minute or less, using her back and legs to support her weight.

As she unstrapped the shotgun from her back in preparation for the climb, a disturbing thought occurred to her—if the person who'd gone through the waterfall *was* one of the S.T.A.R.S., how had they known that the passage was even there?

Good question, and not one she wanted to linger over. Holding the shotgun tightly, Jill pushed the gate open and carefully started down the shaft.

They'd given Barry a full fifteen minutes before heading through the winding halls of the west wing and finding the open back door. They stood there now, looking at the slab of copper and its four engraved crests.

Chris stared at the crescent moon that Barry had taken, feeling confused and more than a little worried. Barry was one of the most honest, straightforward guys that he had ever known. If he said that he was going to look for Jill and then come back for them, then that's what he meant to do.

But he didn't *come back. And if he ran into trouble, how did the piece I gave him end up here?*

He didn't like any of the explanations his mind was giving him to work with. Someone could have taken it from him, he could've placed it himself and then been injured somehow . . . the possibilities seemed endless, and none of them good.

Sighing, he turned away from the diagram and looked at Rebecca. "Whatever happened to Barry, we should go ahead. This may be the only way off the estate."

Rebecca smiled a little. "Fine by me. It just feels good to get out of there, you know?"

"Yeah, no kidding," he said, with feeling. He hadn't even realized how accustomed he'd grown to the cold, oppressive atmosphere of the house until they'd left it. The difference was truly amazing.

They walked through the tidy storage room and stopped at the back door, both of them breathing deeply. Rebecca checked her Beretta for about the hundredth time since they'd left the main hall, chewing at her lower lip nervously. Chris could see how tightly wound she was and tried to think if there was anything she needed to know, anything that would help her if they were forced into a combat situation. S.T.A.R.S. training covered all the basics, but shooting at a video screen with a toy gun was a far cry from the real thing.

He grinned suddenly, remembering the words of wisdom he'd gotten on his first operation, a stand-off with a small group of whacked-out survivalists in upstate New York. He'd been terrified, and trying desperately not to show it. The captain for the mission had been a tough-as-nails explosives expert, an extremely short woman named Kaylor. She'd pulled him aside just before they went in, looked him up and down, and given him the single best piece of advice he'd ever received.

"Son," she'd said, *"no matter what happens—when the shooting starts, try not to wet your pants."*

It had surprised him out of his nervousness, the statement so totally weird that he'd literally been forced to let go of the worst of his fear to make room for it. . . .

"What are you grinning about?"

Chris shook his head, the smile fading. Somehow, he didn't think it would work on Rebecca—and the dangers they faced didn't shoot back. "Long story. Come on, let's go."

They moved out into the calm night air, crickets and cicadas buzzing sleepily in the surrounding woods. They were in a kind of courtyard, high brick walls on either side, an offshoot walkway to their left. Chris could hear rushing water nearby and the mournful cry of a dog or coyote in the distance, a lonely, faraway sound.

Speaking of dogs . . .

There were a couple of them sprawled out across the stones, soft moonlight glistening against their wet, sinewy bodies. Chris edged up to one of them and crouched down, touching its flank. He quickly pulled his hand back, scowling; the mutant dog was sticky and warm, like it had been sheathed in a thick layer of mucous.

He stood up, wiping his hand on his pants. "Hasn't been dead long," he said quietly. "Less than an hour, anyway."

There was a rusted iron gate just past some hedges in front of them. Chris nodded at Rebecca and as they walked toward it, the sound of rushing water increased to a dull roar.

Chris pushed at the gate and it swung open on violently squealing hinges, revealing a huge, cut stone reservoir, easily the size of a couple of swimming pools put together. Deep shadows draped and hung at every side, caused by the seemingly solid walls of murky green trees and lush vegetation that threatened to break through the bordering rails.

They moved forward, stopping at the edge of the

massive pool. It was apparently in the slow process of being drained, the turbulent noise caused by the narrow flow of water through a raised gate on the east side. There wasn't a complete path around the reservoir, but Chris saw that there was a walkway bisecting the pool itself, about five feet below water level. There were bolted ladders at both sides, and the path had obviously been submerged until quite recently, the stones dark with dripping algae.

Chris studied the unusual setup for a moment, wondering how anyone got across when it wasn't being drained. Another mystery to add to the growing list.

Without speaking, they climbed down and hurried across, boots squelching against the slimy stones, a clammy humidity enveloping them. Chris quickly scaled the second ladder, reaching down to help Rebecca up.

The heavily shaded path was littered with branches and pine needles and appeared to border the east end of the reservoir, passing over the open floodgate. They started toward the forced waterfall and had only gotten a few feet when it started to rain.

Plop. Plop plop.

Chris frowned, an inner voice informing him coolly that he shouldn't be able to hear raindrops over the roar of the draining water. He looked up—

—and saw a twisted branch fall from the stretching foliage hanging over the rail, a branch that hit the stones and slid smoothly away—

—*that's not a branch*—

—and there were dozens of them already on the

ground, twisting across the dark stones, hissing and writhing as they fell from the trees overhead.

He and Rebecca were surrounded by snakes.

"Oh, shit—"

Startled, Rebecca turned to look at Chris—and felt cold terror shoot through her, her heart squeezed in its icy grip as she took in the path behind him. The ground had come to life, black shapes coiling toward their feet and dropping from above like living rain.

Rebecca started to raise her gun, realizing numbly that there were too many even as Chris roughly grabbed her arm.

"Run!"

They stumbled forward, Rebecca crying out involuntarily as a thick, writhing body fell across her shoulder, a touch of cool scales against her arm as it slid heavily off and hit the stones.

The path zig-zagged and they ran through the shifting shadows, heels crunching down on rubbery, moving flesh, throwing them off balance. Snakes darted forward to strike at their passing boots as they ran over a steel grate, black, foaming water thundering below, the sound of their boots hitting metal lost to the liquid roar.

Ahead of them, the stones were clearer—but the path also dropped off sharply, a small elevator platform marking its end. There was no place left to go.

They crowded on to the tiny platform and Rebecca snatched at the controls, her breath coming in panicked gasps. Chris turned and fired repeatedly, the shots blasting over the crash of water as Rebecca found the operating button and slammed it down.

The platform shuddered and started to descend, slipping down past rock walls toward a massive, empty courtyard below. Rebecca turned, raising the Beretta to help Chris—

—and felt her jaw drop, her throat locking at the gruesome scene. There had to be hundreds of them, the path almost completely hidden by the slithering creatures, hissing and squirming in an alien frenzy as they struck wildly at each other. By the time she managed to unfreeze, the loathsome sight had risen past eye level and was gone.

The ride seemed to last forever, both of them staring up at the edge of the path they'd left behind, tensely, breathlessly waiting for the bodies to start falling. When the lift was within a few feet of the bottom, they both jumped off, stumbling quickly away from the wall.

They both leaned against the cool rock, gasping. Rebecca took in the courtyard they'd escaped to in between shuddering breaths, letting the sound of the splashing waterfall soothe her nerves. It was a huge, open space made out of brick and stone, the colors washed out and hazy in the frail light. The water from the reservoir above tumbled down into two stone pools nearby, and there was a single gate across from them.

And no snakes.

She took a final deep breath and blew it out, then turned to Chris.

"Were you bit?"

He shook his head. "You?"

"No," she said. "Though if it's all the same to you, I'd rather not go back that way. I'm more of a cat-person, really."

Chris stared at her for a moment and then grinned, pushing away from the wall. "Funny, I would've figured you for lab rats. I—"

Beep-beep.

The radio!

Rebecca grabbed at the unit hooked to her belt, the snakes suddenly forgotten. It was the sound she'd been hoping to hear ever since they'd found Richard. They were being hailed, maybe by searchers—

She thumbed the receiver and held the radio up so they could both hear. Static crackled through the tinny speaker along with the soft whine of a wavering signal.

"... *this is Brad!* ... *Alpha team* ... *read? If* ... *can hear this* ..."

His voice disappeared in a burst of static. Rebecca hit the transmit button and spoke quickly.

"Brad? Brad, come in!"

The signal was gone. They both listened for a moment longer, but nothing else came through.

"He must have gotten out of range," Chris said. He sighed, walking farther out into the open yard and gazing up at the dark, overcast sky.

Rebecca clipped the silent radio back to her belt, still feeling more hopeful than she had all night. The pilot was out there somewhere, circling around and looking for them. Now that they were clear of the mansion, they'd be able to hear him signal.

Assuming he comes back.

Rebecca ignored the thought and walked over to join Chris, who had found another tiny elevator platform, tucked in the corner across from the waterfall. A quick check showed it to be without power.

Chris turned toward the gate, slapping a fresh clip into his Beretta. "Shall we see what's behind door number one?"

It was a rhetorical question. Unless they wanted to go back through the snakes, it was their only option.

Just the same, Rebecca smiled and nodded, wanting to make sure he knew she was ready—and hoping desperately that if anything else happened, she would be.

Fourteen

JILL STOOD AT THE EDGE OF A YAWNING, open pit in the dank tunnel, staring helplessly at the door on the other side. The pit was too wide to safely jump and there was no way to climb down, at least not that she could see. She'd have to go back and try the door by the ladder.

Her frustrated sigh turned into a shiver. The damp chill emanating from the stone walls would have been bad enough without her being dripping wet.

Great secret passage. To use it, you have to catch pneumonia.

A glint of metal caught her gaze as she turned, feet squelching in her boots. She peered down at it, brushing a wet strand of hair out of her eyes. It was a small iron plate set into the stone, a six-sided hole about the size of a quarter at the center. She looked back at the door thoughtfully.

Maybe it works a bridge, or lowers stairs . . . ?

It didn't matter, since she didn't have whatever tool it required, it was as good as a dead end. Besides, it was unlikely that whoever she'd seen walking through the waterfall had managed to get across.

Jill walked back through the twisting passage toward the entrance to the tunnel, still in awe of what she'd found behind the curtain of water. It appeared that there was a whole network of tunnels running beneath the estate. The walls were rough and uneven, chunks of sandy limestone protruding at odd angles—but the sheer amount of work that had gone into creating the underground path was mind-boggling.

She reached the metal door next to the ladder, having to make a conscious effort not to let her teeth chatter as a cold draft swept down from the courtyard above. The sound of the waterfall was strangely muted. The steady, echoing rhythm of water dripping to the rock floor was much louder, giving the tunnels a somewhat medieval feel. . . .

She pulled the door open—and froze, feeling a rush of mixed emotions as Barry Burton whirled around to face her, revolver in hand. Surprise won.

"Barry?"

He quickly lowered his weapon, looking as shocked as she felt—and just about as wet, too. His T-shirt clung to his broad shoulders, his short hair plastered to his skull.

"Jill! How did you get down here?"

"Same way you did, apparently. But how did you know—"

He held up his hand, shushing her. "Listen."

They stood in tense silence, Jill looking up and down the stone corridor and failing to hear whatever Barry had heard. There were metal doors at either end, cast in shadow by the dim utility lights overhead.

"I thought I heard something," he said finally. "Voices . . ."

Before she could ask any questions, he turned and faced her, smiling uneasily. "Look, I'm sorry I didn't wait for you, but I heard somebody walking out in the garden and had to take a look. I found this place by accident, kind of tripped and fell in . . . anyway. I'm glad you're here. Let's check around, see what we can dig up."

Jill nodded, but decided to keep a close eye on Barry for awhile. Maybe she *was* paranoid, but in spite of his words, he didn't seem all that happy to see her. . . .

Watch and wait, her mind whispered. For now, there was nothing else she could do.

Barry led them toward the door to the right, holding his Colt up. He pulled the handle, revealing another gloomy tunnel.

A few steps in to the right was another metal door and across from it, the passage veered sharply into almost complete darkness. Barry motioned at the door and Jill nodded. He pushed it open and the two of them moved in to another silent corridor.

Jill sighed inwardly as she studied the bare rocky

walls, wishing that she had a piece of chalk with her. The tunnel they were in now looked pretty much like all the rest of them, turning left up ahead. She already felt lost, and hoped that there weren't too many more twists and turns—

"Hello? Who's there!" A deep, familiar voice shouted from somewhere ahead of them, the words echoing through the passage.

"Enrico?" Jill called out.

"Jill? Is that you?"

Excited, Jill ran the last few steps to the corner and around, Barry right behind her. The Bravo team leader was still alive, had somehow ended up down here—

Jill rounded the next corner and saw him sitting against the wall, the tunnel widening out and ending in a shadowy alcove.

"Hold it! Stop right there!"

She froze, staring at the Beretta he had pointed at her. He was injured, blood seeping from his leg and puddling on the floor.

"Are you with anyone, Jill?" His dark eyes were narrowed with suspicion, the black bore of his semi-automatic unwavering.

"Barry's here, too—Enrico, what happened? What's this about?"

As Barry stepped out from behind the corner, Enrico stared at them both for a long moment, his gaze darting back and forth nervously—and then he sagged, lowering his gun as he fell back against the stones. Barry and Jill hurried over, crouching down next to the wounded Bravo.

"I'm sorry," he said weakly. "I had to make sure. . . ."

It was as though defending himself had taken his last bit of strength. Jill took his hand gently, alarmed at how pale he was. Blood oozed from his thigh, his pants soaked with it.

"This whole thing was a set-up," he breathed, turning his watering gaze toward her. "I got lost, I climbed the fence, saw the tunnels . . . found the paper . . . Umbrella knew, all along. . . ."

Barry looked stricken, his face almost as white as Enrico's. "Hang on, Rico. We'll get you out of here, you just have lie still—"

Enrico shook his head, still looking at Jill. "There's a traitor in the S.T.A.R.S.," he whispered. "He told me—"

Bam! Bam!

Enrico's body jumped as two holes suddenly appeared in his chest, blood pulsing out of them in violent spurts. Through the resounding echo of the shots, running footsteps clattered away down the corridor behind them.

Barry launched to his feet and sprinted around the corner as Jill helplessly squeezed Enrico's twitching hand, her heart pounding and sick. He slumped over, dead before he touched the cold stone floor.

Her mind flooded with questions as Barry's pursuing footsteps faded away, silence settling once again over the deep shadows. What paper had the Bravo found? When Enrico had said "traitor" she'd immediately thought of Barry, acting so strangely—but he'd been right beside her when the shots had been fired.

So who did this? Who was Trent talking about? Who did Enrico see?

Feeling lost and alone, Jill held his cooling hand and waited for Barry to come back.

Rebecca was going through an old trunk pushed against one wall of the room they'd entered, shuffling through stacks of papers and frowning while Chris checked out the rest of the room. A single, rumpled cot, a desk, and a towering, ancient bookshelf were the only other pieces of furniture. After the cold, alien splendor of the mansion, Chris was absurdly grateful to be in simpler surroundings.

They'd come to a house at the end of the long, winding path from the courtyard, much smaller and infinitely less intimidating than the mansion. The hall they'd stepped into was plain, undecorated wood, as were the two small bedrooms they'd discovered just off the silent corridor. Chris figured they'd found a bunkhouse for some of the mansion's employees.

He had noticed the thick, unmarked dust in the hallway on their way in with a sinking resignation, realizing that none of the other S.T.A.R.S. had made it out of the main house. With no way for him and Rebecca to get back, all they could do was try to find the back door and go for help. Chris didn't like it, but there weren't any other options.

After a brief perusal of the shelves, Chris walked to the battered wooden desk and pulled at the top drawer; it was locked. He bent down and felt along the bottom of the drawer, grinning as his fingers touched a thick piece of tape.

Don't people ever watch movies? The key's always stuck under the drawer. . . .

He peeled the tape away and came up with a tiny silver key. Still grinning, he unlocked the drawer and pulled it open.

There was a deck of playing cards, a few pens and pencils, gum wrappers, a crumpled pack of cigarettes—junk, mostly, the kind of stuff that always seemed to accumulate in desk drawers. . . .

Bingo!

Chris picked up the key ring by its leather tag, pleased with himself. If finding the exit was this easy, they'd be on their way back to Raccoon in no time.

"Looks like we just got a break," he said softly, holding up the keys. The leather tag had the word "Alias" burned into one side, the number "345" written on the back in smudged ball-point pen. Chris didn't know the significance of the number, but he remembered the nickname from the diary he'd found in the mansion.

Thank you, Mr. Alias. Assuming the keys were for the bunkhouse, they were that much closer to getting off the estate.

Rebecca was still sitting by the trunk, surrounded by papers, envelopes, even a few grainy photos that she'd pulled out. She seemed totally absorbed in whatever she was reading, and when Chris walked over to join her, she looked up at him with eyes clouded by worry.

"You find something?"

Rebecca held up the piece of paper she was reading. "A couple of things. Listen to this: 'Four days since the accident and the plant at Point 42 is still growing and mutating at an incredible rate. . . .'"

She skipped ahead, skimming the page with one finger as she spoke. "It calls this thing *Plant* 42, and says its root is in the basement . . . here. 'Shortly after the accident, one of the infected members of the research team became violent and broke the water tank in the basement, flooding the entire section. We think some trace chemicals used in the T-virus tests contaminated the water and contributed to Plant 42's radical mutations. A number of shoots have already been traced to different parts of the building, but the main plant now hangs from the ceiling in the large conference room on the first floor. . . .

"'We've determined that Plant 42 has become sensitive to movement and is now carnivorous. In close proximity to humans, it uses tentacular, prehensile vines to entrap its prey while leechlike adaptations latch onto exposed skin and draw fatal quantities of blood; several members of the staff have already fallen victim to this.' It's dated May twenty-first, signed Henry Sarton."

Chris shook his head, wondering again how someone could invent a virus like the one they had come across. It seemed to infect everything it touched with madness, transforming its carrier into a deadly carnivore, hungry for blood.

God, now a man-eating plant.

Chris shuddered, suddenly twice as glad that they'd be leaving soon.

"So it infects plants, too," he said. "When we report this, we'll have to—"

"No, that's not it," she said. She handed him a photo, her expression grim.

It was a blurry snapshot of a middle-aged man wearing a lab coat. He was standing stiffly in front of a plain wooden door, and Chris realized that it was the very door they'd come through not ten minutes ago—the front entrance to the bunkhouse.

He flipped the picture over, squinting at the tiny script on the back. "H. Sarton, January '98, Point 42."

He stared at Rebecca, finally understanding her fearful gaze. They were standing in Point 42. The carnivorous plant was *here*.

Wesker stood in the darkness of the unlit tunnel, his irritation growing as he listened to Barry stumble through the echoing corridors. Jill wouldn't wait forever, and the raging Mr. Burton couldn't seem to grasp that Enrico's killer had simply slid into the shadows just around the corner, the most obvious place there was.

Come on, come on . . .

Since they'd left the house, he'd finally started to feel like things were going in his favor. He'd remembered the underground room near the entrance to the labs, and was almost certain that the wolf medal would be there. And the tunnels were clear. He had expected the 121s to be out, but apparently no one had messed with the passage mechanisms since the accident. They'd split up to search for the lever that worked the passages—and it had been in plain sight, propped up next to the very mechanism that it controlled.

Everything would have been perfect—except goddamned Enrico Marini had wandered along, happening across a very important paper that Wesker had accidentally dropped—his orders, straight from the head of White Umbrella. And then to complicate matters, Jill had blundered into the tunnels before Wesker could finish taking care of the problem.

Wesker sighed inwardly. If it wasn't one thing, it was another. In truth, this whole affair had been a massive headache from the beginning. At least the underground security hadn't been activated—though he'd had no way of knowing that until they'd reached the tunnels, and having dragged Barry along as insurance, he now had to deal with the consequences. If the money wasn't so good—

He grinned. Who was he kidding? The money was *great*.

After what felt like years, Barry huffed into the dark room, blindly waving his revolver around. Wesker tensed, waiting for him to walk past the generator's alcove. This part could be tricky—Barry and Enrico had been close.

As Barry stormed past the small chamber, Wesker stepped out behind him and jammed the muzzle of his Beretta into Barry's lower back, hard. At the same time, he started talking, low and fast.

"I know you want to kill me, Barry, but I want you to think about what you're doing. I die, your family dies. And right now, it looks like Jill may have to die, too—but you can stop it. You can put a stop to all the killing."

Barry had stopped moving as soon as the gun touched him, but Wesker could hear the barely contained rage in his voice, the pure, driving hatred.

"You killed Enrico," he snarled.

Wesker pushed the gun deeper into his back. "Yes. But I didn't want to. Enrico found some information he shouldn't have, he knew too much. And if he'd told Jill what he knew about Umbrella, I'd have had to kill her, too."

"You're going to kill her anyway. You're going to kill all of us—"

Wesker sighed, allowing a pleading note to creep into his voice. "That's not true! Don't you get it—I just want to get to the laboratory and get rid of the evidence before anyone finds it! Once that material is destroyed, there's no reason for anyone else to get hurt. We can all just . . . walk away."

Barry was silent, and Wesker could tell that he wanted to believe him, wanted desperately to believe that things could be that simple. Wesker let him waver for a moment before pressing on.

"All I want you to do is keep Jill busy, keep her and anyone else you run into away from the labs, at least for a little while. You'll be saving her life—and I swear to you that as soon as I get what I need, you and your family will never hear from me again."

He waited. And when Barry finally spoke, Wesker knew he had him.

"Where *are* the labs?"

Good boy!

Wesker lowered the gun, keeping his expression blank just in case Barry had good night vision. He pulled a folded paper out of his vest and slipped it into Barry's hand, a map from the tunnels to the first basement level.

"If for some reason you can't keep her away, at least go with her. There are a lot of doors with locks on the outside down there; worse comes to worst, you can lock her up until it's over. I mean it, Barry—no one else has to get hurt. It's all up to you."

Wesker stepped back quickly, reaching for the lever with the six-sided tip that he'd left next to the generator. He watched Barry for a few seconds longer, saw the sag in the big man's shoulders, the submissive hang of his head. Satisfied, Wesker turned and walked out of the room. On the very slight chance that any of the S.T.A.R.S. made it to the lab, Mr. Burton would ensure that there wouldn't be any more trouble.

He hurried back through the entrance tunnel, silently congratulating himself on getting things back under control as he headed toward the first passage mechanism. He'd have to move fast from here on out; there were a few things he'd neglected to mention to Barry—like the experimental security detachment that would be released into the tunnels once he turned that lever for the first time. . . .

Sorry, Barry. Slipped my mind.

It would be interesting to see how his team fared with the 121s, the Hunters. Watching the S.T.A.R.S. pit their strength and agility against the creatures would be quite a show—and sadly, one that he'd have to miss.

It was too bad, really. The Hunters had been caged for a long time; they'd be very, very hungry.

FIFTEEN

BARRY HAD BEEN GONE FOR TOO LONG.
Jill had no idea how extensive the tunnels were, but
from what she'd seen they all looked alike. Barry
could be lost, trying to find his way back. Or he could
have found the murderer, and without any back-
up . . .

He might not come back at all.

In any case, staying put wasn't going to help anything. She stood up, taking a last look at the Bravo's
pale face and silently wishing him peace before walking away.

*What did he find out that got him killed? Who was
it?*

Enrico had only managed to get out that the traitor
was a *he,* but that didn't exactly narrow things down;
except for herself and the rookie, the Raccoon

197

S.T.A.R.S. were all male. She could rule out Chris, since he'd been convinced from the start that there was something weird going on—and now Barry, who'd been with her when Marini died. Brad Vickers simply wasn't the type to do anything dangerous, and Joseph and Kenneth were dead—

—*which leaves Richard Aiken, Forest Speyer, and Albert Wesker.*

None of them seemed likely, but she had to at least consider the possibility. Enrico was dead. And she no longer doubted that Umbrella had one of the S.T.A.R.S. in their pocket.

When she got to the door, she quickly leaned down and tightened her damp boot laces, preparing herself. Whoever had shot the Bravo could have just as easily taken her and Barry out—and since he hadn't, she could only figure that he didn't want to kill anyone else, and wouldn't be looking for more targets. Assuming that he was still in the underground system, she'd have to be as quiet as possible if she wanted to find him; the tunnels were perfect sound conductors, amplifying even the tiniest sound.

She eased open the metal door, listening, and then edged out into the dim tunnel, staying close to the wall. In front of her, the corridor was unlit. She opted to head back the way she'd come instead; the darkness was a perfect spot for an ambush. She didn't want to find out she was wrong about the killer's intentions by taking a bullet.

A low, grinding rumble reverberated through the heavy stone walls, a sound like something big moving.

Jill instinctively used the sound as cover, taking several sliding steps forward and reaching the next metal door just as the rumbling stopped. She slipped back out into the tunnel where she'd run into Barry, gently closing the door behind her.

What the hell was that? It sounded like an entire wall moving!

She shuddered, remembering the descending ceiling of that room in the house. Maybe the tunnels were rigged, too; she needed to watch every step. The idea of being crunched to death by some bizarre mechanism underground—

Like the one next to that pit, with the hexagonal hole?

She nodded slowly, deciding that she needed to go take another look at those doors she couldn't get to before. Maybe the killer had the tool it required, and the noise she'd heard had come from him operating it. She could be wrong, but there was no harm in checking. . . .

And at least I won't get lost.

She reached for the door that would lead her back and stopped, her head cocked to catch the strange sound coming from the tunnel behind her. It was—a rusty hinge? Some kind of a bird, maybe? It was loud, whatever it was. . . .

Thump. Thump. Thump.

That sound she knew. Footsteps, headed in her direction, and it was either Barry or someone built like him. They were heavy, plodding—but too far apart, too . . . deliberate.

Get out of here. Now!

Jill grabbed at the metal latch and ran into the next tunnel, no longer caring how much noise she made. Although she sometimes misread them, her instincts were never wrong—and they were telling her that whoever or *whatever* was making that sound, she didn't want to be there when it showed up.

She took several running steps down the stone corridor, away from the ladder that led back to the courtyard—and then forced herself to slow down, taking a deep breath. She couldn't just go sprinting ahead, either; there were other dangers than the one she'd left behind—

Behind her, the door opened.

Jill turned, raising her Beretta—and stared in horror at the thing standing there. It was huge, shaped like a man—but the resemblance stopped there. Naked but sexless, its entire muscular body was covered with a pebbled, amphibious skin, shaded a dark green. It was hunched over so that its impossibly long arms almost touched the floor, both its hands and feet tipped with thick, brutal claws. Tiny, light-colored eyes peered out at her from a flat reptilian skull.

It turned its strange gaze toward her, dropped its wide-hinged jaw—and let out a tremendous, high-pitched screech like nothing she'd ever heard before, the sound echoing around her, filling her with mortal terror.

Jill fired, three shots that smacked into the creature's chest and sent it reeling backwards. It stumbled, fell against the tunnel wall—

—and with another terrible shriek it sprang at her,

pushing off the stones with powerful legs, its claws outstretched and grasping.

She fired again and again as it flew toward her, the bullets tearing into its puckered flesh, ribbons of dark blood coiling away—

—and it landed in a heaving crouch only a few feet in front of her, screaming, one massive arm snaking out to swipe at her legs. A musky, moldy animal smell washed over her, a smell like dark places and feral rage.

—*Jesus why won't it* die—

Jill trained the Beretta on the back of its skull and emptied the clip. Even as the green flesh splattered away and bone splintered, she continued to fire, the hot slugs ripping into the pulpy, pinkish mass of its brain.

Click. Click. Click.

No more bullets. She lowered the weapon, her entire body shaking. It was over, the creature was dead—but it had taken almost an entire clip, fifteen nine-millimeter rounds, the last seven or eight at close range. . . .

Still staring at the fallen monster, she ejected the empty magazine and loaded a fresh clip before holstering the Beretta. She reached back and unstrapped the Remington, taking comfort in the solid, balanced weight of the shotgun.

What the hell were you people working on out here? It seemed that the Umbrella researchers had invented more than just a virus—something just as deadly, but with claws. . . .

And there could be more of them.

She'd never had a more horrifying thought. Holding the Remington close, Jill turned and ran.

Chris and Rebecca walked down a long, wooden hallway, warily glancing up with every other step. There was what looked like dried, dead ivy poking out of every crack and crevice where the walls met the ceiling, a bone-colored growth that scaled across the planks like a fungus. It looked harmless—but after what Rebecca had read to him about Plant 42, Chris kept himself ready to move quickly.

After going through the rest of the papers in the trunk, Rebecca had come up with a report on some kind of an herbicide that could apparently be mixed in Point 42, called V-Jolt. She'd brought it along, though Chris doubted it would be useful. All he wanted was to find the exit, and if they could avoid the killer plant, so much the better.

The front hall had been clear of the growth, though Chris wasn't prepared to call it secured. Besides the two bedrooms by the front door, there had been a rec room that had been distinctly creepy. Chris had looked inside and immediately felt his internal alarms going off, though he hadn't known why; there'd been no danger that he could see, just a bar and a couple of tables. In spite of the seeming calm, he had closed the door quickly and they'd moved on. His gut feeling was enough of a reason to leave it alone.

They stopped in front of the only door in the long, meandering stretch of hallway, both of them still glancing nervously at the scaling ivy near the ceiling. Chris pushed at the knob, and the door swung open.

Warm, humid air flooded out of the shadowy room, thick and tropical—but with a nasty undertone, like the taint of spoiled fruit. Chris instinctively pushed Rebecca behind him as he saw the walls of the chamber. They were completely covered in the same kind of strange, straggling growth that was in the hall—but here, the scaling ivy was lush and bloated, a bilious verdant green.

There was a faint whispering coming from inside the room, a subtle sense of movement—and Chris realized that it was coming from the sickly plant matter itself, the walls quivering in a weird optical illusion as the draping tendrils crept and grew.

Rebecca started to step past him and Chris pushed her back. "What, are you nuts? I thought you said this thing sucks blood!"

She shook her head, staring at the whispering walls. "That's not Plant 42, at least not the part the report talked about. Plant 42 is gonna be a lot bigger, and a lot more mobile. I never did much with phytobiology, but according to that study, we'll be looking for an angiosperm with motile foliage—"

She smiled a quick, nervous smile. "Sorry. Think great big plant bulb with ten to twenty foot vines waving around it."

Chris grimaced. "Great. Thanks for putting my mind at rest."

They edged into the large room, careful not to walk too closely to the hissing walls. There were three doors besides the one they came through: one directly across from the entrance and the other two facing each other to their left, where the room opened up.

Chris led them toward the door opposite the entrance, figuring it as the most likely to lead out of the bunkhouse.

The door was unlocked, and Chris started to push it open—

BAM!

The door slammed shut, causing them both to jump back, weapons raised. A series of heavy, sliding *thumps* followed, like someone on the other side was kicking at the walls—except the sounds were everywhere, above and below the door's sturdy frame, beating against every corner of the sealed room.

"Lots of vines, you said?" Chris asked.

Rebecca nodded. "I think we just found Plant 42."

They listened for a moment, Chris thinking about the kind of strength and weight it would take to slam the door so solidly.

No kidding, bigger and more mobile . . . and maybe blocking the only exit to this place. Terrific.

They backed away, turning into the open area and looking at the other two doors. The one on their right had the number "002" above it. Chris fished out the keys he'd found and flipped through them, finding one with a matching number.

He unlocked the door and stepped inside, Rebecca behind him. There was a smaller door to the left that opened to a bathroom, quiet and dusty. The room itself was another bedroom, a bunk, a desk, a couple of shelves. Nothing of interest.

There was another series of dull thumps from behind the far wall and they quickly moved back into the humid, whispering room, Chris fighting a growing certainty that they were going to have to deal with the plant if they wanted to get out.

Not necessarily, there could still be another way—

The way things had been going so far, he didn't think so. From the shuffling zombies lurking in the main house to the run through the courtyard, snakes dropping from the trees, every part of the Spencer estate seemed to be designed to keep them from leaving.

Chris shook the negative thoughts aside as they approached the shadowy chamber's final door—but they came rushing back at the sight of the small green keypad set next to the frame. He rattled the knob but there was no give. It was another dead end.

"Security lock," he said, sighing. "No way to get in without the code."

Rebecca frowned down at the pattern of tiny red lights set above the numbered buttons. "We could just try numbers until we run across the right combination. . . ."

Chris shook his head. "You know what our chances are of just *stumbling* across the right—"

He stopped, staring at her, then fumbled the key ring out of his pocket.

"Try three-four-five," he said, watching eagerly as Rebecca dutifully punched in the number.

Come on, Mr. Alias, don't fail us now. . . .

The pattern of red lights flashed, then blinked out, one by one. As the last tiny light faded, there was a click from inside the door.

Chris grinned, pushing the door open—and felt his hope dwindle as he glanced around the tiny room.

Dusty shelves filled with tiny glass bottles and a rust stained sink; not the exit he'd expected.

No, that would have been too easy, God knows we can't have that. . . .

Rebecca walked quickly to one of the shelves and looked over the glass bottles, mumbling to herself. "Hyoscyamine, anhydride, dieldrin . . ."

She turned back to him, grinning widely. "Chris, we can kill the plant! That V-Jolt, the phytotoxin—I can make it here. If we can get to the basement, find the plant's root—"

Chris smiled back. "—then we can destroy it without having to fight the damned thing! Rebecca, you're brilliant. How long do you need?"

"Ten, fifteen minutes."

"You got it. Stay here, I'll be back as soon as I can."

Rebecca was already pulling down bottles as Chris closed the door and jogged back toward the corridor, past the whispering walls of shadowy green.

They were going to beat this place, and once they got out, Umbrella was going down hard.

Barry was standing over Enrico's cold body, Wesker's map crumpled in one hand. Jill had been gone when he'd returned—and rather than look for her, he'd found himself unable to move, to even tear his gaze away from the corpse of his murdered friend.

It's my fault. If I hadn't helped Wesker get out of the house, you'd still be alive. . . .

Barry stared miserably at Enrico's face, so filled with guilt and shame that he didn't know what to do anymore. He knew he had to find Jill, keep her from

getting to Wesker, keep his family from being hurt—
but still, he couldn't seem to force himself to walk
away. What he wanted more than anything was to be
able to explain himself to Enrico, make him understand how things had come to be the way they were.

*He's got Kathy and the babies, Rico . . . what else
could I have done? What can I do but follow his orders?*

The Bravo stared back at him with glazed, unseeing
eyes. No accusation, no acceptance, no nothing. Forever. Even if Barry continued to help the captain and
everything else turned out the way it was supposed to,
Rico Marini would still be dead—and Barry didn't
know how he was going to live with the knowledge
that he was responsible. . . .

Shots echoed through the tunnels. A lot of them.

Jill!

Barry's head snapped around. He reached for his
weapon automatically, the sounds spurring him to
action as anger flushed through his system. There
could only be one explanation; Wesker had found Jill.

Barry turned and ran, sick at the thought of another
S.T.A.R.S. member dead by Wesker's treacherous
hand, furious with himself for believing the captain's
lies—

The door in front of him slammed open and Barry
stopped dead in his tracks, all thoughts of Wesker and
Jill and Enrico wiped away by the sight of the crouching thing in front of him. His mind couldn't grasp
what he saw, his stunned gaze feeding him bits of
information that didn't make sense. Green skin.
Piercing, orange-white eyes. Talons.

It screamed, a horrible, squealing cry and Barry

didn't think anymore. He squeezed the trigger and the shriek turned into a bubbling, choking gasp as the heavy round tore into its throat and knocked it down.

The thing flailed its limbs wildly as blood spurted from the smoking hole. Barry heard several sharp cracks like breaking bones, saw more blood pour from its fists as long, thick claws snapped off against rock.

Barry stared in mute astonishment as the creature continued to spasm violently, burbling through the ragged hole in its throat as if still trying to scream. The shot should have blown its head off its neck—but it was another full minute before it died, its frenzied thrashings gradually weakening as blood continued to pump out at a tremendous rate. Finally, it stopped moving—and from the dark, noxious lake it had created, Barry realized that it had bled to death, conscious until the end.

What did I just kill? What the fu—

From the tunnel outside, another shrieking howl resounded through the clammy air—and was joined by a second, then third. The animal cries rose up, furious and unnatural, the screams of creatures that shouldn't exist.

Barry dug into his hip pack with shaking hands and pulled out more rounds for the Colt, praying to God that he had enough—and that those shots he'd heard before hadn't been Jill's last stand.

Sixteen

IT COULD HAVE ONCE BEEN A SPIDER, IF spiders ever got to be the size of cattle. From the thick layer of white web that covered the room, floor to ceiling, it couldn't have been anything else.

Jill stared down at the curled, bristling legs of the abomination, her skin crawling. The creature that had attacked her by the courtyard entrance had been terrifying, but so alien that she hadn't been able to relate it to anything. Spiders, on the other hand . . . she already hated them, hated their dark, bustling bodies and skittering legs. This one had been the mother of all of them—and even dead, it frightened her.

Hasn't been dead long, though. . . .

She forced herself to look at it, at the slick puddles of greenish ichor that dripped from the holes in its

rounded, hairy body. It had been shot several times—
and from the noxious ooze that seeped from the
wounds, she guessed that it had still been alive and
crawling not twenty minutes ago, maybe less.

She shuddered and stepped away toward the double
metal doors that led out of the webbed chamber.
Whispering streams of the sticky stuff clung to her
boots, making it a struggle to move. She took careful,
deliberate steps, determined not to fall. The thought
of being covered in spider web, having it clinging to
her entire body . . . she shuddered again, swallowing
thickly.

Think about something else, anything—

At least she knew she was on the right track, and
close behind whoever had triggered the tunnel mechanism. Neat trick, that. When she'd reached the area
where the pit had been, she'd thought that maybe
she'd gotten lost after all. The gaping hole had been
gone, smooth stone in its place. Looking up, she'd
seen the ragged edges of the pit suspended overhead;
the entire center section of the tunnel had been
flipped over, turned like a giant wheel by some
miracle of engineering.

The doors had led to another straight, empty tunnel. A giant boulder stood at one end, and past that,
the room she was about to leave—

Jill grabbed the handle of one of the doors and
pushed it open, stumbling out into yet another
gloomy passage. She leaned back against the door and
breathed deeply, barely resisting the urge to brush
wildly at her clothes.

I can blow away zombies and monsters with the best

of 'em; show me a spider and I lose my freaking mind. . . .

The short, empty tunnel ran left to right in front of her, a door at either end—but the door to her left was set into the same wall as the one she'd just exited, leading back toward the courtyard. Jill opted for the one on the right, hoping that her sense of direction was still intact.

The metal door creaked open and she stepped in, feeling the change in the air immediately. The tunnel split in front of her. To the right, a thickening of shadow where the rock walls opened into another corridor. But to her left was a small elevator shaft like the ones in the courtyard. A warm, delicious wind swept down and over her, the sweet air like a forgotten dream.

Jill grinned and started for the shaft, seeing that the lift's platform had been taken up. Chances were good that she was still on the trail of Enrico's killer. . . .

. . . but maybe not. Maybe he went the other way, and you're about to lose him.

Jill hesitated, gazing wistfully at the small shaft—and then turned around, sighing. She had to at least take a look.

She walked into the stone corridor that stretched in front of her, the temperature immediately dropping back to the now familiar unpleasant chill. The tunnel extended several feet to her right and dead ended. To her left, a massive, rounded boulder like the one she'd seen before marked the other end, a good hundred feet away. And there was something small laying in front of it, something blue. . . .

Frowning, Jill walked toward the giant rock, trying to make out the blue object. Halfway down the dim tunnel was an offshoot to the left, and she recognized the metal plate next to it as the same kind of mechanism that had moved the pit.

She stepped into the small offshoot, examining the worn stones at its opening. There was a small door to her right, and Jill realized that the passage and room could be hidden by way of the mechanism, the walls turned to block the entrance.

Jeez, it must've taken them years to set all this up. And to think I was impressed with the house. . . .

She opened the door and looked inside. A mid-sized square room of rough stone, a statue of a bird on a pedestal the only decoration. There was no other exit, and Jill felt a sudden rush of relief as the implications sank in. She could leave the underground tunnels; the killer had to have left already.

Smiling, she stepped back out into the corridor and started toward the giant rock, still curious about the blue thing. As she got closer, she saw that it was a book, bound in blue-dyed leather. It had been thrown carelessly against the base of the stone, laying face down and open. She slung the Remington across her back and crouched down to pick it up.

It was a book-box. Her father had told her about them, though she'd never actually seen one. There was a cut-away section of pages behind the cover where valuables could be hidden, though this one was empty. . . .

She flipped it closed, tracing the gold-leaf letters of

the title, *Eagle of East, Wolf of West,* as she started back toward the elevator. Didn't sound like much of a thriller, though it was nicely bound—

Snick.

Jill froze as the stone beneath her left foot sank down a tiny bit—and she realized at the same instant that the entire tunnel gently sloped away from where she was standing.

—oh no—

Behind her, a deep, thundering sound of rock grating against rock.

Dropping the book, Jill sprinted for cover, arms and legs pumping as the rumbling grew louder, the tripped boulder picking up momentum. The dark opening of the offshoot seemed miles away—

—won'tmakeitgonnadie—

—and she could almost *feel* the tons of stone bearing down on her, wanted desperately to look but knew that the split-second difference would kill her. In a final, desperate burst of speed she dove for the opening, crashing to the floor and jerking her legs in—

—as the massive rock rolled past, missing her by inches. Even as she drew in her next gasping breath, the boulder hit the end of the tunnel with an explosive, bone-jarring *crunch* that shook the underground passage.

For a moment, it was all she could do to huddle against the cold floor and not throw up. When that passed, she slowly got to her feet and dusted herself off. The heels of her hands were abraded and both her knees bruised from the running dive, but compared to being smashed flat by a big rock, she thought she had definitely made the right choice.

Jill unstrapped the Remington and headed for the elevator shaft, very much looking forward to leaving the underground behind—and keeping her fingers crossed that whatever came next, it wouldn't be cold. And that there wouldn't be any spiders.

The basement was flooded, all right.

Chris stood at the top of a short ramp that led to the basement doors, staring down at his own unsmiling face reflected off of the shimmering water. It looked cold. And deep.

After he'd left Rebecca, he'd continued down the hall and found room 003 at the end, the ladder to the basement level tucked discreetly behind a bookcase in the neatly kept bedroom. He'd descended into a chilled concrete corridor with buzzing fluorescent lights overhead, a dramatic change from the plain wood and simple style of the bunkhouse above.

At least I found *the basement. . . .*

It appeared that killing Plant 42 was their only option for escape after all. He'd seen no other exit from the bunkhouse, which meant that it had to be past the plant's room—or else there *was* no back door, a thought that left him distinctly unsettled. It didn't seem possible, but then, neither did a carnivorous plant.

And you won't find out until you get this over with.

Chris sighed, and stepped into the water. It *was* cold, and had an unpleasant chemical smell. He waded down to the door, the water sliding up over his knees and finally stopping at mid-thigh, sloshing gently. Shivering, he pushed the door open and moved inside.

The basement was dominated by a giant glass-fronted tank in the center of the room that extended floor to ceiling, a large, jagged hole toward the bottom right-hand side. Chris wasn't that good at judging volume, but to fill the whole area with water, he figured that the tank had to have held several thousands of gallons.

What the hell were they studying that they needed that much? Tidal waves?

It didn't matter; he was cold, and he wanted to find what he needed to find and get back to dry land. He started off toward the left, slowly, straining against the push and pull of the gently lapping waves.

It was totally unreal, wading through a well-lit concrete room, though he supposed it was no stranger than anything else he'd experienced since the Alpha 'copter had set down. Everything about the Spencer estate had a dream-like feel to it, as if it existed in its own reality far removed from the rest of the world's . . .

Try nightmare-like. Killer plants, giant snakes, the walking dead—all that's missing is a flying saucer, maybe a dinosaur—

He heard a soft sloshing behind him and glanced over his shoulder—

—to see a thick, triangular fin rise up from the water twenty feet away and slide toward him, a wavering gray shadow beneath.

Panic shot through him, an all-encompassing panic that seared away rational thought. He took a giant, running step—

—and realized that he couldn't run as he plunged face first into the cold, chemical water and came up gasping, spluttering tainted liquid from his nose and mouth, hoping to God Rebecca was right about the virus having burned itself out.

He whipped his head around, eyes burning, searching for the fin—

—and saw that it had halved the distance between them. He could see it now—a shark, its rippling, distorted body sliding easily through the water, ten or twelve feet long, its broad tail lashing it forward—the black, soulless eyes set above its pointed grin.

—*wet bullets misfire*—

Chris stumbled away backwards, knowing that he didn't stand a chance of outrunning it. Wheeling his arms for balance, he sloshed heavily through the dragging water, turning himself sideways and managing a few more steps before the shark was on top of him—

—and he leaped to the side, dodging the animal and slapping the water as violently as he could, churning it into foaming waves. The shark slid past him, its smooth, heavy body brushing against his leg.

As soon as it was past, Chris stumbled after it, splashing wildly to keep up as he turned the corner in the flooded room. If he could stay close enough, it wouldn't be able to turn, to get at him—

—except that in seconds, the shark would have the room to maneuver. He could see two doors ahead on the left but the giant fish was already leaving him behind, heading toward the next corner to turn around and come back for him.

Chris took a deep breath and plunged into the water, knowing it was crazy but that he didn't have a better chance. He stroked desperately toward the first door, kicking off against the cement floor to propel himself forward in great, bounding leaps.

He hit the door just as the shark was turning up ahead and grabbed for the handle, choking—

—and it was locked.

Shitshitshit—

Chris jammed his hand into his wet vest and came up with Alias's keys, fumbling through them as the fin glided closer, the wide, pointed grin opening—

He shoved a key into the lock, the last key on the ring that he hadn't found the room for, and slammed his shoulder against the door at the same time, the shark now only a few feet away.

The door flew open and Chris stumbled in, falling and kicking frantically. His boot connected solidly with the shark's fleshy snout, deflecting it from the opening. In a flash, he was on his feet. He threw his weight into the door and in a slap of water, it was closed.

He sagged against the door, wiping at his stinging eyes with the back of his hand. The lapping water settled gently into smaller and smaller ripples as he caught his breath and his vision cleared. For now, he was safe.

He unholstered his Beretta and ejected the dripping

magazine, wondering how the hell he was going to make it back upstairs. Looking around the small room, he saw nothing he could use as a weapon. One wall was lined with buttons and switches, and he trudged over to look at them, drawn to a blinking red light in the far corner.

Looks like I found a control room . . . aces. Maybe I can turn off the lights and get the shark to go to sleep.

There was a lever set next to the flashing light and Chris stared down at the faded tape beneath it, feeling a numb disbelief as he read the printed letters.

Emergency Drainage System.

You've gotta be kidding me! Why didn't anyone pull this thing the second the tank broke?

The answer occurred to him even as he thought it. The people who worked here were scientists; no way they were going to turn down the opportunity to study their precious Plant 42, sucking up water from the man-made lake.

Chris grabbed the lever and pushed it down. There was a sliding, metallic noise outside the door—and immediately, the water level started to drop. Within a minute, the last of it had flowed out from under the door and a gurgling, liquid gasp came from the direction of the broken tank.

He walked back to the door, opening it carefully— and heard the frantic, wet *thumps* of a very big fish trying to swim through air.

Chris grinned, thinking that he should probably feel

pity for the helpless creature—and hoping instead that it died a long, agonizing death.

"Bite me," he whispered.

Wesker had shot four of the shuffling, gasping Umbrella workers on his way to the computer room on level three. He hadn't recognized any of them, though he was pretty sure that the second one he'd taken out had been Steve Keller, one of the guys from Special Research. Steve always wore penny loafers, and the pallid, dried-up husk that had reached for him by the stairs had been wearing Steve's brand.

It appeared that the effects of the viral spill had been harsher in the labs . . . less messy, but no less disquieting. The creatures that roamed the halls outside seemed to have been totally dehydrated, their limbs withered and stringy, their eyes like shriveled grapes. Wesker had dodged several of them, but the ones he'd been forced to put down had scarcely bled at all.

He sat at the computer in the cool, sterile room and waited for the system to boot up, feeling truly on top of things for the first time all day. He'd had earlier moments, of course. The way he'd handled Barry, finding the wolf medal in the tunnels—even shooting Ellen Smith in the face had given him a momentary sense of accomplishment, a feeling that he was in control of what was happening. But so much had gone wrong along the way that he hadn't had time to enjoy any of his successes.

But now I'm here. If the S.T.A.R.S. aren't already dead, they will be soon—and assuming I don't suffer some massive lapse of skill, I'll be out of here within half an hour, mission complete—

There were still dangers, but Wesker could handle them. The mesh monkeys—the Ma2s—were undoubtedly loose in the power room, but they were easy enough to get past, as long as you didn't stop running; he should know, he'd helped come up with the design. And there was the big man, the Tyrant, waiting one level down in his glass shell, sleeping the sweet, dreamless sleep of the damned. . . .

. . . *From which he'll surely never wake. What a waste. So much power, crossed off as a failure by the boys at White. . . .*

A gentle musical tone informed him that the system was ready. Wesker pulled a notebook out of his vest and opened it to the list of codes, though he already knew them; John Howe had set the system up months ago, using his name and the name of his girlfriend, Ada, as access keys.

Wesker tapped out the first of the passwords that would allow him to unlock the laboratory doors, feeling a sudden, vague wistfulness for the excitement of the day. It would be over so soon and there would be no one to witness his achievements, to share his fond memories after the fact.

Now that he thought about it, it was a shame that none of the S.T.A.R.S. would be joining him; the only thing better than a grand finale was a grand finale with an audience. . . .

SEVENTEEN

JILL HAD TAKEN THE ELEVATOR INTO WHAT
seemed to be another part of the garden or courtyard,
although the area had been isolated, surrounded by
trees; she'd guessed as much from the few overgrown
potted plants and the welcome sounds of the forest
beyond the low metal railing. There had been nothing
to see but a rusting door set into a nondescript,
overgrown wall, welded shut—and a large, open well,
like a stone wading pool. Inside had been a short,
spiral staircase leading down to another small elevator.

Which I took—but now where the hell am I?

The room that the elevator had led to was unlike
any other part of the estate she'd seen. It lacked the
strange, fetid charm of the mansion, or the dripping
gloom of the underground. It was as though she'd

walked out of a gothic horror story and into a military complex, a utilitarian's bleak paradise.

She was standing in a large, steel-reinforced concrete room, the walls painted a muddy industrial orange. Metal ducts and overhead pipes lined the upper walls, and the room was rather aptly titled "XD-R B1," painted across the concrete in black, several feet high. Any sense she'd had of where she was in relation to the rest of the estate was totally gone.

Although it's as cold as everywhere else, at least I know I'm still on the grounds. . . .

There was a heavy metal door on one side of the room, firmly locked. The sign to the left of it stated that it was only to be opened in case of a first-class emergency. She figured that the "B1" on the wall stood for "Basement level one," her theory confirmed by the bolted ladder that led down through a narrow shaft in the concrete; where there was B1, B2 naturally followed.

And considering the alternative, it looks like that's where I'm headed. My other option is to go back through the underground tunnels.

She peered down the ladder shaft, only able to see a square of concrete at the bottom. Sighing, she held on to the Remington and started down.

As soon as she hit the last rung, she turned anxiously—and faced a much smaller room, as bland and industrial as the first. Inset fluorescent lights on the ceiling, a gray metal door, concrete walls and floor. She walked through quickly, starting to feel hopeful that there were no more creatures or traps. So far, the basement levels had offered nothing more dangerous than a lack of decorum. . . .

She opened the door and her hope faded as the dry, dusty smell of long-dead flesh hit her. She stepped out onto a cement walkway that led over a flight of descending stairs, a metal railing circling the path. At the top of the steps was a crumpled zombie, so emaciated and shriveled that it appeared mummified.

She held the shotgun ready and walked slowly toward the stairs, noting that there was a hall branching off to the left where the railing stopped. She darted a quick look around the corner and saw that it was clear. Still watching the desiccated corpse carefully, she edged down the short corridor and stopped at the door on her left. The sign next to the door read "Visual Data Room," and the door itself was unlocked.

It opened up into a still, gray room with a long meeting table in the center, a slide projector set up in front of a portable screen at the far end. There was a phone on a small stand pushed up against the right wall, and Jill hurried over, knowing that it was too much to hope for but having to check just the same.

It wasn't a phone at all, but an intercom system that didn't seem to work. Sighing, she stepped past an ornamental pillar and walked around the table, glancing at the empty slide projector. She let her gaze wander, looking for anything of interest—

—and it stopped on a flat, featureless square of metal set into the wall, about the size of a sheet of paper. Jill stepped over to take a closer look.

There was a flat bar at the top. She touched it

lightly, and the panel slid down into the wall, revealing a large red button. She looked around the quiet room, trying to imagine what the trap would be—and then realized that there wouldn't be a trap at all.

The mansion, the tunnels—all of it was rigged to keep people from getting here, to these basement levels. They're way too efficiently dull to be anything but where the real work gets done.

She knew instinctively that her logic was sound. This was a board room, a place for drinking bad coffee and sitting through meetings with colleagues; nothing was going to jump out at her if she pushed the button.

Jill pushed it. And behind her, the ornamental pillar slid to one side with a smooth, mechanical hum. Behind the pillar were several shelves, stacked with files—and something that glittered in the soft gray light of the room.

She hurried over and picked up a metal key, the top of it imprinted with a tiny lightning bolt. Slipping it into her pocket, she flipped through a few of the files. They were all stamped with the Umbrella logo, and though most of them were too thick and ponderous to spend time sorting through, the title on one of the reports told her what she needed to know, what she'd already suspected.

Umbrella / Bioweapons Report / Research and Development.

Nodding slowly, Jill put the file back. She'd finally found the *real* research facilities, and she knew that the S.T.A.R.S. traitor would be somewhere in these rooms. She was going to have to be very careful.

With a final glance around her, Jill decided to go see if she could find the lock that the key belonged to. It was time to place the last few pieces of the puzzle that Umbrella had set up and that the S.T.A.R.S. had sacrificed themselves trying to solve.

The twisted, gnarled root of Plant 42 took up a large corner of the basement room, the bulk of it hanging down in slender, fleshy tendrils that almost touched the floor. A few of the tiny, worm-like threads squirmed blindly around each other, twisting slowly back and forth as if looking for the water supply that Chris had drained.

"God, that's *disgusting,*" Rebecca said.

Chris nodded agreement. Besides the control room he'd escaped into, there had only been two other chambers in the basement. One of them had been stacked with boxes of cartridges for all kinds of weapons—and although most of them had been uselessly wet, he'd found most of a box of nine-millimeter rounds on a high shelf, saving them both from running out of ammunition.

The other room had been plain, containing only a wood table, a bench—and the massive, creeping root of the carnivorous plant that lived upstairs.

"Yeah," Chris said. "So how do we do this?"

Rebecca held up a small bottle of purplish fluid and swirled it gently, still staring at the moving tendrils. "Well, *you* stand back, and don't breathe too deeply. This stuff's got a couple of toxins in it that neither of us want to be ingesting, and it'll turn gaseous once it hits the infected cells."

Chris nodded. "How will we know if it's working?"

Rebecca grinned. "If the V-Jolt report is on the mark, we'll know. Watch."

She uncapped the bottle and stepped closer to the twisted root—then upended the glass vial, dousing the snaking tendrils with the watery fluid.

Immediately, a billow of reddish smoke plumed up from the root as Rebecca emptied the bottle and stepped quickly away. There was a hissing, crackling sound like wet wood thrown atop a blazing fire—and within seconds, the feebly twisting fibers started to break, pieces of them snapping off and flaking away. The knotted thickness at the center started to tighten and shrink, pulling into itself.

Chris watched in amazement as the giant, terrible root suddenly shriveled up into a dripping ball of mush no bigger than a child's ball and hung there, dead. The entire process had taken about fifteen seconds.

Rebecca nodded toward the door and both of them stepped out into the drying basement, Chris shaking his head.

"God, what'd you put in there?"

"Trust me, you don't want to know. You ready to get out of here?"

Chris grinned. "Let's do it."

They both jogged toward the basement doors, hurrying out into the cold corridor and back toward the ladder that led upstairs. Chris was already going over escape plans for when they left the bunkhouse. It really would depend on where the exit led. If they ended up in the woods, he was thinking that they should head toward the closest road and light a fire, then wait for help to come. . . .

. . . though maybe we'll get lucky, run across the damned parking lot for this place. We can hotwire a car and drive out—and get Irons to do something useful for a change, like call in reinforcements. . . .

They reached the wood corridor and headed for the plant room, both of them taking long, easy strides past the hissing green walls and finally stopping at the room that held Plant 42.

Breathing deeply, Chris nodded to Rebecca. They both unholstered their weapons and Chris pushed the door open, eager to see what lay beyond the experimental plant.

They stepped into a huge, open room, the smell of rotting vegetation thick in the damp air. Whatever it had looked like before, the monster that had been Plant 42 was now a massive, steaming lake of dark purple goo in the center of the room. Bloated dead vines the size of fire hoses draped limply across the floor, extending out from the livid, gelid mass.

Chris scanned for the next door, saw a plain fireplace against one wall, a broken chair in a corner—

—and a single door that apparently led *back* into the bedroom he'd searched earlier. A hidden passage that he'd missed—and that led to the very room in which they stood.

Must have been behind the bookcase. . . .

There was no way out. Killing the plant had been a waste of time, it hadn't been blocking anything.

Rebecca looked as disappointed as he felt, her shoulders slumped and expression grim as she studied the bare walls.

Ah, I'm sorry, Rebecca.

They both walked slowly around the room, Chris staring at the dead plant and trying to decide what to do next. Rebecca walked to the fireplace and crouched down next to it, poking at the blackened ash.

He wouldn't drag her back to the mansion, neither of them were up for it. Even with the extra ammo, there were too many snakes. They could wait in the courtyard for Brad to fly by again, hope he got into range—

"Chris, I've found something."

He turned and saw her pull a couple of pieces of paper out of the ashes, the edges scorched but both sheets otherwise intact. He walked across the room and leaned down to read over her shoulder—and felt his heart start pounding as the first words sank in.

SECURITY PROTOCOLS

BASEMENT LEVEL ONE:

Heliport/For executive use only. This restriction may not apply in the event of an emergency. Unauthorized persons entering the heliport will be shot on sight.

Elevator/The elevator stops during emergencies.

BASEMENT LEVEL TWO:

Visual Data Room/For use by the Special Research Division only. All other access to the Visual Data Room must be cleared with Keith Arving, Room Manager.

BASEMENT LEVEL THREE:

Prison/Sanitation Division controls the use of the prison. At least one Consultant Researcher (E. Smith, S. Ross, A. Wesker) must be present if viral use is authorized.

Power Room/Access limited to Headquarters Supervisors. This restriction may not apply to Consultant Researchers with special authorization.

BASEMENT LEVEL FOUR:

Regarding the progress of "Tyrant" after use of T-Virus . . .

The rest of the paper was burned, the words lost.

"A. Wesker," Chris said softly. "Captain Albert goddamn *Wesker . . .*"

Barry had said that Wesker disappeared right after the Alphas had made it to the house. *And it was Wesker who led us here in the first place when the dogs attacked. Cool, competent, unreadable Wesker, working for Umbrella. . . .*

Rebecca flipped to the second page and Chris leaned in, studying the neatly typed labels beneath the drawn boxes and lines.

MANSION. COURTYARD. GUARDHOUSE. UNDERGROUND. LABORATORIES.

There was even a compass drawn next to the sketch of the mansion, to show them what they'd missed—a secret entrance to the underground hidden behind the waterfall.

Rebecca stood up, eyes wide and uncertain. "Captain Wesker is involved with all this?"

Chris nodded slowly. "And if he's still here, he's down in those labs, maybe with the rest of the team. If Umbrella sent him here, God only knows what he's up to."

They had to find him, had to warn whoever was left of the S.T.A.R.S. that Wesker had betrayed them all.

Everything was done. Wesker stepped into the elevator that led back to level three, running through his checklist as he lowered the outer gate and slid the inner one closed.

. . . samples collected, disks erased, power reconnected, Tyrant support off . . .

It was really too bad about the Tyrant. Ugly as it was, the thing was a marvel of surgical, chemical, and genetic engineering, and he'd stood in front of its glass chamber for a long time, studying it in silent awe before reluctantly shutting down its life support. As the stasis fluids had drained, he'd found himself imagining what it would have been like to see it in action once the researchers had completed their work. It would have been the ultimate soldier, a thing of beauty in the battlefield . . . and now it had to be destroyed, all because some idiot tech had hit the wrong button. A mistake that had cost Umbrella millions of dollars and killed the researchers who had created it.

He hit the switch and the elevator thrummed to life, carrying him back up for his final task—activating the triggering system at the back of the power room. He'd give himself fifteen minutes to make sure he was clear of the blast radius, climb down the heliport ladder, hit the back road toward town—and boom, no more hidden Umbrella facility. At least not in Raccoon Forest. . . .

Once he got back into the city, he'd pack a bag and head for Umbrella's private air strip. He could make the necessary calls from there, let his contacts in the White office know what had happened. They'd have a clean-up team standing by to comb through the forest and take out the surviving specimens—and they'd be most eager to get their hands on the tissue samples he'd taken, two of everything except for the Tyrant. With the Tyrant scientists all dead, Umbrella had decided to shelve the project indefinitely. Wesker thought it was a mistake, but then, he wasn't getting paid to think.

As the elevator slid to a stop, Wesker opened the gates and stepped out, setting down the sample case. He unholstered his Beretta, going over the twisting layout of the power room in his mind. He had to make another run through the Ma2s to get to the activation system. He'd already managed it once to hook up the elevator circuit, but they had been more active than he'd expected; instead of weakening them, their hunger had driven them to new heights of viciousness. He'd been lucky to make it through unscathed—

At a hydraulic hum from down the hall, Wesker froze. Footsteps clattered across the cement floor, hesitated—and then started for the power room at the opposite end of the corridor.

Wesker eased up to the corner and looked down the hall, just in time to see Jill Valentine disappear through the metal doors, a burst of hissing mechanical noise echoing through the corridor before they closed.

How did she make it through the Hunters? Jesus!

Apparently he'd underestimated her . . . and she'd been alone, too. If she was that good, the Ma2s might not kill her, and she had effectively just blocked him from the triggering system. He wouldn't be able to deal with the creatures that roamed the maze-like walkways *and* put a stop to her prying. . . .

Frustrated, Wesker scooped up the sample case and walked quickly down the hall, back toward the hydraulic doors that led to the main corridor of level three. If she made it back out, he'd just have to shoot her; it would only delay his escape by a few minutes. Still, it was an unexpected curve, and as far as he was concerned, it was too late in the game for surprises. Surprises pissed him off, they made him feel like he wasn't in control. . . .

I AM in control, nothing is happening here that I can't handle! This is MY game, my rules, and I will accomplish my mission without any interference from that little thief-bitch—

Wesker stalked out into the main corridor, saw that Jill had managed to take out a few more of the wizened, withered scientists and technicians that wandered the basement labs. Two of them lay just outside the door, their skulls blown into arid powder by what looked like shotgun blasts. He kicked one of them angrily, his boot crunching into the corpse's brittle ribs, the dry *snap* of bone loud in the silence—

—except that suddenly, he heard heavy boots coming down the metal stairs from B2, the hollow *clump* echoing through the hall. And then a rough, hesitant voice calling out.

"Jill?"

Barry Burton, as I live and breathe—

Wesker raised his weapon coolly, ready to fire when Barry stepped into view—and then lowered it thoughtfully. After a moment, a slow grin spread across his face.

Eighteen

JILL EASED INTO THE STEAMING, HISSING room, a thick smell of grease in the heated air. It was some kind of a boiler room, and a big one; heavy, thrumming machinery filled the large chamber, surrounded by winding catwalks. Massive turbines spun and pounded, generating power in a steady whine as hidden ducts spat out steam at short intervals.

She moved slowly into the poorly lit chamber, peering down one of the railed walkways into the fluctuating shadows cast by the towering generators. From where she was, she could see that the place was a labyrinth of paths, twining around the giant blocks of noisy machinery.

The source of the estate's power. That explains how they managed to keep it a secret for so long, they had their own little city out here, totally autonomous— probably had their food shipped in, too. . . .

She turned down the narrow walk to her right, watching uneasily for any more of the strange, pale zombies that she'd seen in the corridors of B3. The path seemed clear, but with the movement and noise created by the turbines—

Something ripped at her left shoulder, a sudden, violent slash that tore open her vest and scraped the skin beneath.

Jill spun and fired, the roar of the shotgun drowning out the hissing machines. The blast hit metal, pellets ricocheting into the empty walk. There was nothing behind her.

Where—

A lunging, blade-like claw sliced the air in front of her face, swooping down from above.

She stumbled back, staring up at the steel mesh of the ceiling—and saw a dark shape skitter out of the shadows, hooking its way across the grate incredibly fast, curving claws at its hands and feet. She caught a glimpse of thick spines around its mutant, flattened face and then it turned and ran into the thrumming shadows of the power room.

There was a door at the end of the walk and Jill sprinted toward it, heart racing, the pounding whine of the generators thundering in her ears.

She was five feet from the door when she saw the moving shadow position itself in front of her. She raised the shotgun and leaned back—

—more of them!

There were two of the creatures overhead, squat, terrible things with vicious, curving hooks instead of hands. One of them dropped down suddenly, hanging by clawed feet to swipe at her with its bladed arm.

Jill fired and the creature screeched, the blast hitting it in the chest. It fell from the ceiling with a clatter, thick blood oozing out of the ragged wound.

She turned back toward the entrance and ran, hearing the patter of claws against the mesh overhead. Another of the aberrant monkey-like things swung down in front of her, and Jill ducked, afraid to stop running. The thing's strange arm whistled past her ear, missing her head by less than an inch.

The metal doors were in front of her. Jill crashed into them, slapping one handle down and stumbling back into the cold stillness of the corridor. The door closed on the furious, shrill cry of one of the monsters, rising high over the sounds of the working machines.

She sagged against the door, gasping—

—and saw Barry Burton standing midway down the chilled, silent hall. He hurried toward her, an expression of deep worry on his rugged, bearded face.

"Jill! Are you alright?"

She pushed away from the door, surprised. "God, Barry, where have you been? I thought you'd gotten lost in the tunnels."

Barry nodded grimly. "I did. And I ran into some trouble trying to get out."

She saw the splatters of blood on his clothing, the rips and tears in his shirt, and realized that he must have come across more of those walking green nightmares. He looked like he'd been through a war.

Speaking of . . .

Jill touched her shoulder, her fingers coming away bloody. It was painful but shallow; she'd survive.

"Barry, we've got to get out of here. I found some papers upstairs, proof of what's been going on. Enrico was right, Umbrella's behind all of this and one of the S.T.A.R.S. knew about it. It's too dangerous to keep looking around, we should get those files and head back to the mansion, wait for the RPD—"

"But I think I found the main lab," Barry said. "Downstairs, there's an elevator at the end of the hall. There are computers and stuff. We can get into their files, really nail 'em."

He didn't seem excited by the find, but Jill barely noticed. With the information they could get from Umbrella's database: names, dates, research material—

We can find out everything, present the investigators with the whole, messy package. . . .

Jill nodded, grinning. "Lead the way."

The tunnels had been a cold, miserable maze, but the map had led them through quickly. Rebecca and Chris had reached the first basement level, both of them shivering and wet—and not a little freaked out by the dead creatures they'd passed along the way. The Umbrella scientists had been disgustingly creative in their approach to making monsters.

Chris rattled the door that supposedly led to the heliport, but it was solidly locked, an emergency sign next to it implying that it could only be opened by an alarm system. He'd hoped to send Rebecca out with the radio while he searched for the others.

He looked down the narrow stairwell and sighed, turning to her. "I want you to stay here. If you stand by the elevator, you should be able to pick up Brad's signal from outside. Tell him where we are and what happened—and if I'm not back in twenty minutes, get back to the courtyard and wait there until help comes."

Flustered, Rebecca shook her head. "But I want to go with you! I can take care of myself, and if you find the lab, you'll need me to tell you what you're looking at—"

"No. For all we know, Wesker already killed the other S.T.A.R.S. and is looking to finish the job. If we're the last ones, we can't risk both of us getting ambushed. Somebody has to survive and tell people about Umbrella. I'm sorry, but it's the only way."

He smiled at her, putting a hand on her shoulder. "And I know you can take care of yourself. This isn't about your competence, okay? Twenty minutes. I just have to see if anyone else made it."

Rebecca opened her mouth as if to protest further and then closed it, nodding slowly. "Okay, I'll stay. Twenty minutes."

Chris turned and started down the ladder, hoping he could keep his promise to come back. The captain had successfully deceived them all, acting the part of concerned leader for weeks while the people in Raccoon City had died—and all along he'd known why. The man was a sociopath.

It seemed that Umbrella had created more than one kind of monster. And it was time to find out how much damage he'd done.

Barry couldn't bring himself to look at Jill as they took the elevator down to B4. Wesker would be waiting for them at the bottom, and Jill would find out that he had been helping the captain all along.

He'd killed three more of the violent, springing creatures down in the tunnels before making it to the lab—only to run into Wesker, who had insisted that he lure Jill down to B4 and assist him in locking her up. The smiling bastard had reminded Barry of his family's situation and promised again that it was the last thing he'd have to do, that after Jill was safely locked away he'd call his people off—

—*except he's said that every time. Find the crests and you're free. Help me in the tunnels, you're free. Betray your friend . . .*

"Barry, are you okay?"

He turned to her as the elevator stopped, looking miserably into her concerned, thoughtful eyes.

"I've been worried about you ever since we got to the mansion," she said, laying a hand across his arm. "I even thought—well, never mind what I thought. Is something wrong?"

He pulled the gate open and raised the mesh outer door, an excuse to look away. "I—yeah, something's wrong," he said quietly. "But now's not the time. Let's just get this over with."

Jill frowned but nodded, still looking concerned. "Okay. When this is over, we can talk."

You won't want to talk to me when this is over. . . .

Barry stepped out into the short hallway and Jill followed, their boots clanking across a steel grate. The hall turned to the left just ahead and Barry slowed down on the pretense of checking his weapon, letting Jill get in front of him.

They turned the corner and Jill froze, staring into the muzzle of Wesker's raised Beretta. He grinned at them, his sunglasses hiding his eyes, his smile smug and leering.

"Hello, Jill. Nice of you to drop by," he said smoothly. "Nice work, Barry. Take her weapons."

She turned her startled gaze to him as he quickly plucked the shotgun from her hands, then reached around to unholster her Beretta, his face burning.

"Now get back up to B1 and wait for me by the exit. I'll be up in a few minutes."

Barry stared at him. "But you said you just wanted to lock her up—"

Wesker shook his head. "Oh, don't worry. I'm not going to hurt her, I promise. Now get going."

Jill looked at him, confusion and fear and anger playing across her face. "Barry?"

"I'm sorry, Jill."

He turned and walked around the corner, feeling defeated and ashamed—not to mention terrified for Jill. Wesker had promised, but Wesker's word meant nothing. He'd probably kill her as soon as he heard the elevator doors close—

—but what if I'm not in the elevator? Maybe I can still do something to keep her alive. . . .

Barry hurried to the lift and opened the gates—

then slammed them closed and pushed the operation switch, sending it back to B3 without a passenger. Moving silently, he edged back toward the corner, listening.

". . . can't say I'm all that surprised," Jill was saying. "But how did you get Barry to help you?"

Wesker laughed. "Ol' Barry's got some trouble at home. I told him that Umbrella has a team watching his house, waiting to kill his precious family. He was only too happy to help."

Barry clenched his fists, his jaw tight.

"You're a bastard, you know that?" Jill said.

"Maybe. But I'm going to be a rich bastard when all this is over. Umbrella is paying me a lot of money to clean up their little problem, and to get rid of a few of you goddamn snooping S.T.A.R.S. in the process."

"Why would Umbrella want to destroy the S.T.A.R.S.?" Jill asked.

"Oh, not all of them. They've got big plans for some of us, at least those of us that want to make a profit. It's you sniveling do-gooders that they don't want—the red-white-and-blue, apple pie, all that happy bullshit. The way Redfield's been running around, mouthing off about conspiracies—you think Umbrella didn't notice? It has to stop, here. This whole place was rigged to blow up just in case of an accident—and the Tyrant virus escaping qualifies. Once you're all dead and this facility's destroyed, no one will be able to get to the truth."

Son-of-a-bitch was *going to kill all of us*—

"But enough about Umbrella. I had you brought down here for a little experiment of my own. I want to see how our most agile team member stands up against the miracle of modern science. If you'll just step through that door—"

Barry flattened himself against the wall as Wesker stepped back, part of his shoulder coming into view. He put his hand on his Colt and drew it out slowly.

"I can't believe that you're doing this," Jill said. "Selling out to protect a bunch of unethical corporate blackmailers—"

"Blackmailers? Oh, you mean Barry. Umbrella wouldn't bother with blackmail. They can afford to buy people just as easily. I made all that up to get him on board—"

Barry slammed the butt of his Colt into Wesker's skull as hard as he could, dropping him like a ton of bricks.

Nineteen

JILL STARED IN ASTONISHMENT AS WESKER suddenly stopped talking and crumpled to the floor—and Barry stepped into view, staring down at Wesker's body with a look of intense hatred, Colt in hand.

She crouched down next to Wesker and pried the Beretta from his fingers, tucking it into her waistband.

Barry turned to look at her, his eyes swimming with apology. "Jill, I'm so sorry. I never should have believed him."

Jill stared at him for a moment, thinking about his daughters. Moira was Becky McGee's age. . . .

"It's okay," she said finally. "You came back, that's what matters."

Barry handed her back her weapons, and they both

gazed down at Wesker's sprawled form, still breathing but unconscious. He was out cold.

"I don't suppose you have any handcuffs on you?" Barry asked.

Jill shook her head. "Maybe we should check out the lab, there's bound to be some cable or cord we can use. Besides, I'm kind of curious about this 'miracle of modern science' he was talking about. . . ."

She turned and found the switch that operated the hydraulic door, noting the bio-hazard symbol painted across the front. The door slid open and the two of them stepped inside.

Wow . . .

It was a huge, high-ceilinged chamber lined with monitoring consoles, cables snaking across the floor and connecting to a whole series of standing glass tubes. There were eight of the tubes lined up in the center of the room, each of them big enough to hold a grown man. They were all empty.

Barry reached down and scooped up a handful of cable, digging into his pocket for a knife while Jill walked toward the back, gazing at the technical and medical equipment—and stopped, staring, feeling her jaw drop.

Against the back wall was a much larger tube, at least eight or nine feet tall, hooked up to its own computer console—and the thing inside filled it, top to bottom. It was monstrous.

"Jill, I got the cable. I—"

Barry stopped next to her, his words faltering as he saw the abomination. Silently, they both walked toward it, unable to resist a closer look.

It was tall, but proportionally correct, at least through the broad, muscular torso and long legs; those parts appeared human. One of its arms had been altered into a cluster of massive, dragging claws, hanging past its knees, while the other seemed ordinary, if overly large. There was a thick, bloody tumor protruding from where its heart would be, and Jill realized, staring at the bulbous mass that it *was* the thing's heart; it was pulsing slowly, expanding and contracting in slow, rhythmic beats.

She stopped in front of the tube, awed by the abomination. She could see lines of scar tissue snaking across its limbs, surgical scars. It had no sexual organs; they'd been cut away. She looked up at its face and saw that parts of the flesh there had also been removed; the lips were gone, and it seemed to grin broadly at her through the sliced red tissue of its face, all of its teeth exposed.

"Tyrant," Barry said quietly.

Jill glanced over at him, saw him frowning down at the computer that was hooked to the tube by multiple cables.

She looked back at the Tyrant, feeling nearly overwhelmed by pity and disgust. Whatever it was now, it had once been a man. Umbrella had turned him into a freakish horror.

"We can't leave it like this," she said softly, and Barry nodded.

She joined him at the console, looking down at the myriad switches and buttons. There had to be a switch that would put an end to its life; it deserved that much.

There was a set of six red switches in a row along the bottom and Barry flipped one of them down. Nothing seemed to happen. He glanced at her, and she nodded for him to continue. He used the side of his hand to flip all of them.

There was a sudden, dull *thump*—

They both whirled around, saw the Tyrant pull back its human hand and hit the glass again. Cracks webbed out from the impact, though the glass had to be several inches thick—

"Oh . . . *SHIT!*"

Barry grabbed her arm as the creature drew its bleeding knuckles back for another blow.

"Run!"

They ran, Jill wishing to God that they'd left it alone, panic welling up from deep inside of her. Barry slammed his hand down on the door control and it slid open as behind them, glass shattered.

They stumbled through the door, terrified, Barry hitting the lock—

—and saw that Wesker was gone.

Wesker stumbled toward the power room, his head pounding, his limbs feeling strangely distant and weak. He felt like he was going to throw up.

Goddamn Barry . . .

They'd taken his gun. He'd come to as they'd walked into the lab and reeled toward the elevator, cursing them both, cursing Umbrella for creating such a screwed up mess, cursing himself for not simply killing the S.T.A.R.S. when he could have.

It's not over. I'm still in control. This is my game. . . .

The sample case was down in the lab, probably being destroyed right now by one of those idiots. Tyrant, too. That magnificent creature, powerless without the adrenaline injections, dead. They'd shoot him in his sleeping heart, he'd die without ever tasting battle. . . .

Wesker reached the door to the room and leaned against it, struggling to catch his breath. Blood dribbled out of his ears and he shook his head, trying to clear it of the strange fog that had settled into his brain.

He didn't have the tissue samples, but he could still complete his mission. It was important, very important that he complete his mission. It was about control, and control was his game.

. . . triggering system, watch out for monkeys . . .

The Ma2s, he had to be careful. Wesker opened the door and pitched forward, the ground seeming too far away and then too close. The machines were hissing at him, whining and hissing in the hot, oily air. His hand found the railing and he pulled himself toward the back of the room, trying to hurry but finding that his legs weren't interested.

A claw shot down from above and tore into his scalp, yanking away a clump of hair. He felt warm liquid trickle down the back of his neck and stumbled on, the pain in his head sharper now.

Took my gun, stupid, stupid assholes took my gun. . . .

He reached the door and had just managed to get it open when something heavy landed on his back, knocking him into the next room. He fell on the cold metal floor and a terrible shriek sounded in his ear. Thick talons punctured the skin on his back and Wesker slapped at it, at the grinning, screaming thing that was trying to kill him.

He hit the creature as hard as he could, shoving the heel of his hand into its throat. It leaped away, landing on the mesh wall and clambering back up to the ceiling.

Wesker pulled himself up and stumbled on, fresh waves of pain and nausea washing over him. The air was too hot, the turbines loud and relentless in their spinning, throbbing frenzy—but he could see the door to the back now, the door that led to the completion of his mission.

All of the S.T.A.R.S., dead, blown into orbit while I escape, fly away a rich man. . . .

He flung the door open and made his way toward the small, glowing screen in the back corner. It was quieter here, cooler. The massive machines that filled the chamber hummed softly at him, their purpose quite different than that of the ones outside. These were the machines that wanted to help him regain his control.

The noise from the open door behind him seemed far away as he reached the glowing screen, his fingers numb as they touched the keyboard beneath.

He found the keys he needed, the code spilling out across the monitor in soft green after only a few mistakes. A sexy, quiet voice informed him that the countdown would begin in thirty seconds. Dizzy, he tried to remember the setting for the timer. The system would trigger automatically in five minutes, but he had to reset it, give himself time to get reoriented and make his way to the outside—

Behind him, something screamed.

Wesker whirled around, confused—and saw four of the mesh-monkeys running at him, lashing out with long, curved hands as they reached him. Terrible pain shot up through his legs and he fell, crashing to the hard steel floor.

This can't happen.

One of the creatures jumped onto his chest and suddenly Wesker couldn't breathe, couldn't even raise his weak arms to push it away. Another tore into his left leg, ripping away a thick chunk of flesh with its hooked claw. The third and fourth screamed in savage glee, dancing around him like dark, vicious children, lifting their claws as they pranced on squat legs.

Somehow, there was blood in his eyes, and the world was spinning away, screams and hisses and incredible, searing heat blurring his vision, his mind—

Tyrant has come.

Wesker could feel it, could feel the presence of something vast and powerful touching him. Grinning through the pain, he searched for it through the red haze of his failing vision, wanting more than anything to see it slaughter his attackers in a glory of perfect motion—but he could only make out the immense shadow that seemed to flood over him, *through* him, could only imagine that the powerful, magnificent warrior was reaching down to lift him from his torment—

I control let me seeeee—

Darkness stole his hopes away, and Wesker thought no more.

"... *S.T.A.R.S. Alpha team, Bravo,* anybody—*if you can't answer, try to signal! I'm running out of fuel, do you read? This is Brad! Repeat—S.T.A.R.S. Alpha team* ..."

Rebecca hit the button, talking fast. "Brad! There's a heliport at the Spencer estate, you have to get to the heliport! Brad, come in!"

There was a high, whining squeal and Rebecca heard what must have been the word *"copy"*—but the rest was lost.

"I copy"? Or, "Do you copy?"

There was no way to know. Frustrated and worried, Rebecca held on to the radio tightly, hoping that he'd heard her.

Suddenly, a shrill alarm blared into the silent room through some hidden speaker in the ceiling. Rebecca jumped, staring around the cold chamber helplessly. There was a buzzing click from inside the door that led to the heliport and she hurried over, grabbing the handle and pulling it open. It had unlocked.

A cool, female voice began to speak, slowly and clearly over the jangling alarm.

"The triggering system has now been activated. All personnel must evacuate immediately or process deactivation. You have five minutes. The triggering system has now been activated—"

As the recorded message repeated, Rebecca stood in the open doorway and watched the open ladder shaft, her blood racing, waiting to see Chris emerge from the levels below.

He'd only been gone a few minutes, but their time had just run out.

Twenty

JILL AND BARRY RAN FROM THE ELEVATOR back toward the main hall of B3, the cool voice informing them that they had four and a half minutes. They hit the open corridor at a dead run, sprinting around the corner—

—and saw Chris Redfield halfway up the metal stairs.

"Chris!" Jill shouted.

He spun around, his face lighting up as he saw them dashing toward him.

"Hurry!" he shouted. "There's a heliport on B1!"

Thank God!

Chris waited until they reached the base of the stairs and then ran ahead, rushing around the walkway and holding open the door that led to the ladder. Jill and Barry made it to the top and sped through, the computer telling them that they had four minutes, fifteen seconds to get away.

Barry went up the ladder first and Jill followed, Chris right behind. They piled out into B1. Jill saw that Rebecca Chambers was standing at the emergency exit, her youthful face tight with anxiety.

Chris hustled her through the door and the four of them ran through a winding concrete hall, Jill praying silently that they'd have time to clear the estate.

I hope you burn here, Wesker.

There was a large elevator at the end of the corridor and Barry slammed the gate open, holding it as they rushed inside. He jumped in after them. They had four minutes even.

The elevator seemed to crawl upward and Jill looked at her watch, heart pounding as the seconds ticked past.

Not gonna make it, we'll never make it—

The lift hummed to a stop and Chris yanked the gate open, the cool air of early morning sweeping over them—and the sweet, wondrous sound of a helicopter overhead, circling.

"He heard me!" Rebecca shouted, and Jill grinned, feeling a sudden wave of affection for the rookie.

The helicopter port was huge, the wide, flat space surrounded by high walls, a circle of yellow paint on the asphalt showing Brad where to set down. Barry and Chris both waved their arms frantically, signaling the pilot to hurry as Jill looked at her watch again. A little over three and a half minutes remained. More than enough time—

CRASH!

Jill whirled around, saw chunks of concrete and tar
fly into the air and rain down over the northwest
corner of the landing pad. A giant claw stretched up
from the hole, fell across the jagged lip—

—and the pale, hulking Tyrant leaped out onto the
heliport, rose smoothly from its agile crouch . . . and
started toward them.

What the hell is that?

It had to be eight feet tall, parts of its giant body
mutilated and deformed, its grinning face focusing on
them even as it stood up. It moved toward them at a
slow walk, the massive claw of its left arm flexing.

No time, Brad can't land—

Chris targeted the dark, tumorous thing on its chest
and fired, pulling the trigger five times in rapid
succession, three of the rounds finding their mark.
The other two were within an inch of the pulsing
redness—

—and the creature didn't even slow down.

"Scatter!" Barry yelled.

The S.T.A.R.S. split, Jill pulling Rebecca to the
farthest corner from the towering monster, Chris
sprinting toward the southern wall. Barry stood his
ground, pointing his Colt at the approaching beast.

Three .357 rounds slammed into its belly, the
thundering shots echoing against the high concrete
walls.

The creature suddenly sped up, running toward
Barry, drawing its giant claw back—

—and as Barry dove out of the way, the thing swept
past him in a running crouch, bringing its claw up as if

throwing a ball underhand. Its talons gouged the asphalt, ripping through it as though it was no more solid than water.

As soon as the monster was past, it stopped running, turning almost casually back to watch Barry scramble to his feet and fire again.

The bullet took out a fleshy chunk of its right shoulder. Thick blood coursed down its wide chest and joined the dripping, open mass of its stomach.

Overhead, the Alpha 'copter still circled, unable to land—and there was still no sign that the immense creature felt the injuries. It started its run again, dropping its terrible, inhuman hand down as it went for Barry—just as his revolver clicked on empty.

Barry sprinted away, but the charging monster veered with him—

—and its sweeping claw glanced against his side, tumbling him to the ground.

Barry!

Chris raced toward the creature, firing into its back as it bent down over the fallen Alpha. Barry was scrambling backwards, his vest shredded, his eyes wide with terror—

—and it must have felt the sting of the bullets because it turned, fixing its emotionless stare on Chris. Barry staggered to his feet and limped quickly away.

We don't have any time!

Chris emptied the clip, the last several rounds hitting it in the face. Pieces of tooth flew from the creature's lipless mouth, spattering to the asphalt in a rain of white and red. The creature didn't seem to notice as it started to run toward him at incredible speed.

Jill and Rebecca were both firing, shouting, trying to turn its attention away from Chris but it was already fixated, pounding toward him and drawing its claw back—

—*wait for it*—

He dove to the side at the last possible second and the monster went flying past, its claw mulching the asphalt where he'd just been standing.

Chris ran, the horrible awareness dawning on him that the seconds were slipping past and that they couldn't kill it in time.

Barry felt blood seeping from his thigh, the top several layers of his skin sliced neatly away by the Tyrant's brutal swipe. The pain was bearable; the knowledge that they were going to die wasn't.

We'll blow up if we don't get chopped to pieces first—

Tyrant turned its attention to Jill and Rebecca, both of them firing again at the seemingly invulnerable monster. It started its smooth, easy walk toward them, still indifferent to the bloody holes in its body. Shotgun blasts hit it in the legs and chest, nine millimeter bullets speckled its pasty flesh, and it didn't falter, kept on walking.

Wind whipped down over Barry as the roar of the helicopter's blades suddenly got louder. He heard a screaming shout come from above.

"Incoming!"

Barry stared up at the 'copter, hovering only twenty feet from the ground—

—and saw a heavy black object fly out of the open door on the side, hitting the tar with an audible *thud*.

Chris was closest. He ran for it.

The Tyrant had almost reached Jill and Rebecca. The two of them split, each headed in a different direction and the creature turned toward Jill without hesitating, tracking her with its strange, fixed gaze.

"Jill, this way!" Chris screamed.

Barry spun—and saw that Chris had the bulky rocket launcher propped on his shoulder.

Yes!

Jill veered toward Chris, the Tyrant close behind.

"Clear!"

She leaped to one side and rolled as Chris fired, the *whoosh* of the rocket-propelled grenade almost lost to the thundering beat of the 'copter's rotors.

The explosion wasn't. The grenade hit the Tyrant square in the chest—and in a burst of incendiary light and deafening sound, it blew the monster into a million smoking pieces.

Even as tattered shreds of flesh and bone hailed down over them, Brad lowered the 'copter back toward the ground and the four S.T.A.R.S. ran for it. The rails hadn't touched yet as Jill dove into the open cabin, Chris and Rebecca and Barry all throwing themselves in after her.

"Go, Brad, now!" Jill screamed.

The bird lifted into the air and sped away.

†wenty-One

THE CALM, FEMALE VOICE FELL ONLY ON inhuman ears.

"You have five seconds, three, two, one. System activation now."

A circuit that ran the length and width of the estate connected.

With an earth-shaking thunderclap of motion and sound, the Spencer estate exploded. Devices went off simultaneously in the basement of the mansion, beneath the reservoir, behind a plain, uninteresting fireplace in the guardhouse and in the third level of the basement laboratories. Marble walls tumbled down over the disintegrating floors of the fine old mansion. Rock collapsed and concrete blew into a fine blackened dust. Massive fireballs rose up into the early morning sky and could be seen from miles away in their few brief seconds of brilliant life.

As the incredible peal of booming sound rolled across the forest and died away, the wreckage started to burn.

EPILOGUE

THE FOUR OF THEM WERE QUIET AS BRAD
piloted the 'copter back toward the city, and though
he had a million questions, something about their
silence didn't invite conversation. Chris and Jill were
both staring out the hatch window at the spreading
fire that had been the estate, their expressions grim.
Barry was slumped against the cabin wall, looking
down at his hands like he'd never seen them before.
The new girl was quietly moving among them, treating their wounds without saying a word.

Brad kept his mouth shut, still feeling crappy about
taking off earlier. He'd been through hell since then,
flying around in circles and watching the fuel gauge
slowly drop. It had been a total nightmare, and he had
to take a piss like nobody's business.

And then that monster—

He shuddered. Whatever it had been, he was glad it was dead. It had taken all of his nerve not to fly away the second he'd laid eyes on it—and as far as he was concerned, he deserved a little consideration for managing to kick the launcher out the door.

He glanced back at the silent foursome, wondering if he should tell them about the weird call he'd gotten over the radio. Right after the rookie had screamed something about a heliport through the static, a clear, solid signal had come in, a male voice calmly giving him the exact coordinates. The guy had been listening in, which was weird—but the fact that he knew the location well enough to give Brad directions was downright spooky.

He frowned, trying to remember the mystery man's name. Thad? Terrence?

Trent. That's it, he said his name was Trent.

Brad decided that it would keep for another day. For now, he just wanted to go home.

About the Author

S.D. (Stephani Danelle) Perry writes multimedia novelizations in the fantasy/science-fiction/horror realm for love and money, including several *Aliens* novels, the novelization of *Timecop* and the soon-to-be-released movie thriller, *Virus.* Under the name Stella Howard, she's written an original novel based upon the television series *Xena, Warrior Princess.* The *Resident Evil* books mark her first foray into writing novels based upon video games. She lives in Portland, Oregon, with her husband and a multitude of pets.

The fight against Umbrella continues in

RESIDENT EVIL

CALIBAN COVE

**The first *all-original*
RESIDENT EVIL novel!
by S.D. Perry**

Available now!

"You must be Rebecca Chambers," he said. He had a British accent, his words clipped and somehow polished. "You're the biochemist, is that right?"

Rebecca nodded. "Working on it. And you are . . ."

He smiled wider, shaking his head. "Forgive my manners, please. I hadn't expected . . . that is, I . . ."

He stepped around Barry's low coffee table and extended his hand, flushing slightly. "I'm David Trapp, with the S.T.A.R.S. Exeter branch in Maine," he said.

Rebecca felt cool relief wash over her; the S.T.A.R.S. had sent help instead of calling, fine by her. She shook his hand, stifling a grin, knowing that her appearance had thrown him. Nobody expected an eighteen-year-old scientist, and while she'd gotten used to the surprised looks, she still took a kind of mischievous pleasure at catching people off guard.

"So, are you like the scout or something?" she asked.

Mr. Trapp frowned. "Sorry?"

"For the investigation—are there other teams already here, or did you come to check things out first, get the dirt on Umbrella . . ."

She trailed off as he shook his head slowly, almost sadly, his dark eyes glittering with an emotion she couldn't read.

It came out in his voice, heavy with frustrated anger—and as the words sank in, Rebecca felt her knees go watery with a sudden anxious dread.

"I'm sorry to have to tell you this, Ms. Chambers. I have reason to believe that Umbrella has gotten to key members of the S.T.A.R.S., either by bribery or blackmail. There is no investigation— and no one else is coming."

A look of confused terror passed through the girl's light brown eyes and just as quickly was gone. She took a deep breath and blew it out.

"Are you sure? I mean, did Umbrella try to get to you, or . . . are you *positive?*"

David shook his head. "I'm not absolutely certain, no—but I wouldn't be here if I wasn't . . . concerned about it."

It was a bit of an understatement, but David still wasn't past the shock of seeing how young she was, and felt an almost instinctive desire not to alarm her any further. Barry had mentioned that she was something of a child genius, but he hadn't really expected a *child*. The biochemist wore high tops and cut-off denim shorts rolled at the knee, topped by a shapeless black T-shirt.

Get past it; this child may be the only scientist we have left.

The thought rekindled the anger that had been burning in David's gut for the past few days. The story that had been unfolding since Barry's call wasn't a pretty one, filled with treachery and lies—and the fact that the S.T.A.R.S., *his* S.T.A.R.S. were involved . . .

Barry walked into the room with a glass of water and Rebecca took it from him gratefully, swallowing half of it in one gulp.

Barry shot him a glance and then turned his attention to Rebecca. "He told you, huh?"

The girl nodded. "Do Jill and Chris know?"

"Not yet. That's why I called," Barry said. "Look, no point in going through this twice. We should wait for them to show up before we get into specifics."

"Agreed," David said. He generally found that first impressions were the most telling, and if they were going to be working together, he wanted to get a feel for the girl's character.

The three of them sat, and Barry started to tell Rebecca how he and David had met back in S.T.A.R.S. training when they were both much younger men. Barry told a good story, even if it was only to kill time. David listened with half an ear as Barry related an anecdote about their graduation night, involving a rather humorless drill sergeant and several rubber snakes. The girl was relaxing, even enjoying the story of their childish prank—

—*seventeen years ago. She would have been celebrating her first birthday.*

Still, she had put her questions on hold at Barry's request, even though David knew she had to be anxious about what he'd told her. The ability to retrain one's focus so quickly was an admirable trait, one that he'd never fully mastered.

He'd been able to think of little else since his own call to the S.T.A.R.S. AD. David's devotion to the organization had made the apparent betrayal all the more bitter, like a bad taste in his mouth that wouldn't go away. The S.T.A.R.S. had been David's life for almost twenty years, had given him all the things he'd lacked growing up—a sense of self-worth, a sense of purpose and integrity. . . .

And just like that, the lives of dedicated men and women, my *life and life's work simply tossed aside as if it meant nothing. How much did that cost? How much did Umbrella have to pay to buy the S.T.A.R.S.'s honor?*

David shook the anger, focusing his attention on Rebecca. If all he'd learned was true, time was short and their resources were now severely limited. His motivations weren't as important right now as hers.

He could tell by the way she held herself that she

wasn't the shy or submissive type, and she was obviously bright; her eyes fairly sparkled with it. From what Barry had told him, she'd acted professionally throughout the Spencer facility operation. Her file suggested that she was more than qualified to work with a chemical virus, assuming that she was as good as the reports said—

—and assuming she has any desire to put her life in further danger.

That was going to be the sticking point. She hadn't been with the S.T.A.R.S. for very long, and knowing that they'd sold their people out probably wasn't going to overwhelm her with feelings of confidence for the job ahead. It would be just as easy for her to step out of the game now. For that matter, it would be the intelligent choice for all of them—

There was a knock at the door, presumably the other two Alphas. David's hand drifted down to the butt of his nine-millimeter as Barry went to answer. When he walked back in leading the S.T.A.R.S. team members, David relaxed, then stood up to be formally introduced.

"Jill Valentine, Chris Redfield—this is Captain David Trapp, military strategist for the Maine S.T.A.R.S. Exeter branch."

Chris was the marksman, if David remembered correctly, and Jill something of a covert B&E specialist. Barry said that the pilot, Brad Vickers, had skipped town shortly after the Spencer incident. No great loss, from what he could gather; the man sounded distinctly unreliable.

He shook hands with both of them and they all sat down, Barry nodding toward him.

"David's an old comrade of mine. We worked together on the same team for about two years, right after boot camp. He showed up on my doorstep about an hour ago with news, and I didn't think it could wait. David?"

David cleared his throat, trying to focus on the significant facts. After a pause, he began at the beginning.

"As you already know, six days ago, Barry placed several calls to various S.T.A.R.S. branches to see if any word had come from the home office about the tragedy that occurred here. I received one of those calls. It was the first I'd heard about it, and I've since found out that the New York office hasn't contacted anyone about your discovery. No warnings or memos. Nothing has been issued to the S.T.A.R.S. regarding the Umbrella Corporation."

Chris and Jill exchanged looks of concern.

"Maybe they're not done investigating," Chris said slowly.

David shook his head. "I spoke to the assistant director myself the day after Barry called. I didn't tell him about the contact, only that I'd heard rumor of a problem in Raccoon, and wanted to know if it had any merit. . . ."

He looked at the assembled group and sighed inwardly, feeling like he'd already gone over it a thousand times.

Only in my mind, searching for another answer . . . and there isn't one.

"The AD wouldn't tell me anything outright," he continued, "and he told me that I should remain quiet about it until official word came down. What he *would* say was that there had been a helicopter crash in Raccoon City—and what he implied was that the surviving S.T.A.R.S. were trying to lay blame on Umbrella, angry over some sort of funding dispute."

"But that's not true!" Jill said. "We were investigating the murders, and found—"

"Yes, Barry told me," David interrupted. "You found that the murders were the result of a laboratory accident. The T-Virus that Umbrella was experimenting with was released somehow and it transformed the researchers into mad killers."

"That's exactly what happened," Chris said. "I know it sounds nuts, but we were there, we *saw* them."

David nodded. "I believe you. I have to admit, I was skeptical after speaking with Barry. As you say, it sounds 'nuts'—but my call to New York and what's happened since has changed all that. I've known Barry for a long time, and I knew that he wouldn't be looking to place blame for such an unfortunate incident unless Umbrella was, in fact, responsible. He even told me about his own unwilling involvement in the attempted cover up."

"But if Tom Kurtz told you that there was no conspiracy . . . ." Chris said.

David sighed. "Yes. We have to assume that either our own organization has been misled—or that, like your Captain Wesker, members of the S.T.A.R.S. are now working for Umbrella."

There was a moment of shocked silence as they absorbed the information, and David could see anger and confusion play across their faces. He knew how they felt. It meant that the S.T.A.R.S. directors had either been manipulated by Umbrella or corrupted by them—and either way, the survivors of the Raccoon team had been hung out to dry, left vulnerable to whatever Umbrella might do.

David glanced around the room, trying to assess their readiness for the rest of it. Barry's fists were clenched, and he stared at them as if he'd never seen them before. Jill and Rebecca both seemed lost in thought, though he could see that they had accepted his story as truth. It would save them time, at least. . . .

Chris stood up and started to pace, his youthful features flushed with anger. "So basically, we've got no credibility with the locals, no backup coming, and we've been branded as liars by our own people. The Umbrella investigation is dead and we're *screwed*, does that pretty much sum it up?"

David could see that the anger wasn't directed at him, just as the anger that *he* felt wasn't for the young Alpha. The thought of what Umbrella had done, what the S.T.A.R.S. were involved in—it made him sick with rage, with feelings of helplessness that he hadn't felt since his childhood.

Stop thinking of yourself. Tell them the rest.

David stood up and looked at Chris, though he addressed all of them. He hadn't even had time to tell Barry yet.

"Actually, there's more. It seems that there's another Umbrella facility on the Maine coast, conducting experiments with this virus of theirs— and just like what happened here, they've lost control."

David turned to Rebecca, taking in her wide, horrified gaze as he finished. "I'm taking a team in, without S.T.A.R.S. authorization—and I want you to come with us."

RESIDENT EVIL™

ORIGINAL SOUNDTRACK REMIXES

Available NOW!

RESIDENT EVIL
CAPCOM
ORIGINAL SOUND
2

RESIDENT EVIL
CAPCOM
VIZ MUSIC
ORIGINAL SOUNDTRACK REMIX
1
S

- Resident Evil™ 2 Soundtrack
- 31 nightmare tracks in full stereo!
- $16.95
- Available Nov. '98.

- Resident Evil™ 1 Soundtrack
- 34 stereo tracks of terror!
- $16.95

Groove with your favorite Ghoulies!

Coming Soon – Street Fighter Alpha 2 and Night Warriors: Darkstalkers' Revenge

Order online www.j-pop.com or call (800) 394-3042 for a (free) catalog

Ask for Viz soundtracks at your local music, game, or comic store!

VIZ MUSIC™

© 1998 Capcom Co., Ltd. All Rights Reserved.

Visit
❖ **Pocket Books** ❖
online at

www.SimonSays.com

Keep up on the latest new
releases from your favorite
authors, as well as author
appearances, news, chats,
special offers and more.

SIMON & SCHUSTER
A VIACOM COMPANY
www.SimonSays.com

Pocket
Books

2381-01